AGAINST THE LOWER TIER OF CABINETS ON THE LEFT SIDE OF THE ROOM, SOMEONE—A HUMANOID FIGURE—LAY CRUMPLED.

Dark blue blood was spattered around and smeared on the cupboard door. Dr. Beverly Crusher knelt beside the faintly breathing shape. "It's an Alpheccan," she said, scanning the inert figure. He wore a dark coverall, the upper right side of which was smeared and sodden with blue from a gaping chest wound. The normal navy blue of his skin was paled almost to cerulean. His eyes were open, two violet orbs looking sightlessly beyond the medical team. There wasn't a hint of consciousness in those eyes.

Commander William Riker shivered.

STAR TREK
THE NEXT GENERATION®

INTELLIVORE

DIANE DUANE

POCKET BOOKS

New York   London   Toronto   Sydney   Tokyo   Singapore

An *Original* Publication of POCKET BOOKS

POCKET BOOKS, a division of Simon & Schuster Inc.
1230 Avenue of the Americas, New York, NY 10020

This book is published by Pocket Books, a division of Simon & Schuster Inc., under exclusive license from Paramount Pictures.

ISBN: 0-671-56832-9

First Pocket Books printing April 1997

10 9 8 7 6 5 4 3 2 1

POCKET and colophon are registered trademarks of Simon & Schuster Inc.

Printed in the U.S.A.

For the "Eastern Bloc":
Andreas, Martin, Astraid, Melanie, Mark,
and all our other acquaintances in Germany and
Switzerland, around *stammtischen* here and there,
who think first of *Raumschiff Enterprise*
before translating it into that slightly alien term,
Star Trek

Cogito, ergo sum.

—Descartes

INTELLIVORE

Chapter One

JEAN-LUC PICARD was out riding. The horse was not his usual mount, but a big bay gelding named Rollo, a soft-mouthed, even-tempered creature. For this ride, the horse would have to be.

It was the third leg of his ride, now, the third day in the saddle, and his muscles were beginning to complain at a strain to which they had become unaccustomed. *Sloppy of me,* he thought, *to let myself get so far out of trim. But we're sorting that out now!* As he reined in again, catching his breath at the twinge in the thigh muscles, Rollo snorted softly: impatience. This was a horse that liked the hard climbs, and would get impatient with a rider who couldn't keep his pace.

"All right," Picard said under his breath, amused. "All right, you beast; we'll see who's the

1

first to call it quits." He shook the reins. Rollo tossed his head and started upward again.

The route was a familiar one, though it had been years since he'd rode it last. The first leg meant an early-morning escape from St.-Veran—otherwise the unwelcome sounds of traffic and town life would put the horse out of humor—and the initial, fairly steep climb up through the meadows outside town, to the hiking trail that struck southeast, skirting the peak of Pointe des Marcellettes.

Once on the trail, things settled into the comfortable rhythm that Picard so relished. He could feel the movement of the horse, and hear the sound of hoofbeats, his own breathing, the wind, and the rush of the Aigue Blanche river paralleling the trail. Northward, the jagged crestline of Pic Traversier dominated the view, its flanks shaggy with pines down to the valley level; and below that, the water meadows surrounding the river course, bright with the violet and yellow of the spring pre-Alpine flowers, early mallow, and wild vanilla orchid. Behind, if he had looked over his shoulder, Picard would have had no trouble seeing the valleys and lesser peaks of the Hauts-Alpes falling away gradually through the bright mist toward the central lowlands. But he didn't look that way. His attention and anticipation were directed toward the eastward road, where the trail zigzagged upward toward the border, and the clear view ahead was shut away by the interlaced fingers of stone that reached down to the trail from one peak or another of the Queyras range through which he traveled.

Picard rode on, too relaxed and happy even to smile. Every now and then the stillness was broken—a rockfall, turned loose by expansion in the warming day, and skittering down the scree slope above the red tile roofs of Marbre village; a little school of Alpine choughs wheeling overhead, stooping down at the trail to dive-bomb the lone rider, so that Picard had to shout to scare them off, and Rollo tossed his head and snorted in annoyance.

But such interruptions were few. The mist burned off, the wind died down; except for the crunch of Rollo's hooves on the scree and gravel of the trail, the silence grew intense in the heat of the bright blue day.

Picard sighed in sheer pleasure at the completeness of that silence as he and Rollo rounded the spur of Tête de Longet, and the view abruptly opened out northeastward, showing the narrow valley running back and forth in the shadow of the jagged heart peaks of the Queyras. Here the trail ceased to be any good for vehicles, and the only comment the maps would make about its quality further on was a laconic *"passage incertain."* Picard drew rein where the narrowing trail passed the old hikers' hut under Pic de Caramantran, and eyed the path above them with pleasure and anticipation. They had gained about two thousand feet over the morning's climb; the sun was still hot, but the air was growing cooler, and in shadow it was cold enough to provoke shivers.

They climbed. Even the insanely hardy Alpine flowers gave up trying to grow here; the Arolla pines had given up a thousand feet earlier. Everything in sight was scree tumble, sloped gravel, blinding patches and streaks of snow, slick shining trickles of ice down gray- and brown-striped, crooked-layered limestone and mica schist, and above it all, the inward-leaning *aiguillette* peaks— barren stone needles like the newest, sharpest mountains on some moon. The sheer sterility of the scenery would have been oppressive had it not been backed by that hard, brilliant blue sky, getting clearer all the time as the trail wound on upward above the last of the mist.

Picard's chest began to hurt. Behind him, Rollo was blowing hard. "Aha," Picard said, between his own gulps for air. *"Now* we see what you—really think of a good climb—" The trail was almost at a forty-degree angle now and, above them, seemed simply to go straight up into the sky and stop.

Until they came to the top of it. Abruptly, almost unbelievably—so great was the contrast with the surrounding terrain—they found themselves standing on a stony crest which spilled straight down into a broad grassy terrace, almost perfectly flat. Picard led Rollo down into it, and the gelding made a satisfied muttering noise down in his throat and immediately dropped his head to graze. "Glutton," Picard said softly, throwing the reins over Rollo's head and letting them hang. He leaned against the horse's side and regarded the view from Belvedere la Cirque with a completely illogical satisfaction, as if he had created it.

Picard left Rollo where he was for the moment and walked slowly to the eastern side of the belvedere, where it began to trend gently downhill before ending abruptly in its own set of cliffs. There, poised on the very edge, he stood awhile, getting his breath back, and looked down into the great soft abyss of blue air to the place below where four or five wrinkled little valleys met. Picard stood there in the sunny silence, awed as always, and thought of how many others had come this way in their own times, on their way to some pressing engagement: Hannibal, Julius Caesar, Napoleon . . .

Except that none of them had actually come *here* at all.

It was all an illusion, of course. The air, so cold and dry and sweet it cut the lungs; the faint elusive scent of vanilla orchid, even at such a height; the clink and creak of the tack of reins and saddle, the faint grinding noise of Rollo's teeth as he grazed, even Rollo himself as he paused in his grazing to look up and snort softly at Picard, impatient with the sightseeing—all an illusion. All the triumph of science over an empty room.

Unreal, Picard thought a little sadly, folding his

arms, now that his breathing was comfortable again. *Yet*—and the thought was almost rebellious, even cheerful—*it's easy enough to get caught in the old question. Any reality must be filtered through our own experience. I may say to myself, "This is unreal: I'm in the holodeck, and a word from me will break the illusion." But it* feels *no less real than the last time I rode this way.*

Picard sighed, amused; but the amusement had an edge of sorrow to it. The irony was inescapable: holodeck technology, rather than helping solve questions about the nature of reality, had created many more. Meanwhile, was there *really* any danger in experiencing this morning sun, this air, as if it *were* physically real? Joy was rare enough, precious enough in life, as it was; why deny it to yourself because it wasn't "real"? Reality would intrude soon enough, and then—

—the soft *queep* from the commbadge buried inside the saddle pack. Picard's slight, glad smile turned wry. "Picard," he said softly.

"Captain," Riker's voice said, *"Marignano* has just come out of warp and is on her way to the rendezvous point."

"Thank you, Number One," Picard said. "My compliments to Captain Maisel. I'll be along shortly. Any news of *Oraidhe* yet?"

"Not yet, sir."

"All right. Out."

He stood there a few minutes more, looking

across the blue lake of air toward Monte Viso's splendor. A black dot slid across the mountain face at about the twenty-five-hundred-meter level, below the peak, its shadow sliding along in a matching course down on the snows. Picard peered at it, for there was something odd about the shape, lumpy.

It had to come a little closer, veering past the face of Pointe de Marte, before he recognized it, and the sight made him catch his breath. Big broad wings, flapping surprisingly and looking black against the blazing white, except for faint pale patches on the shoulders—it was one of the Alpine eagles, the "Imperial eagle" in fact, once rare in these skies. They had been hunted nearly to extinction in the eighteenth and nineteenth centuries; but with the aid of cloned and natural breeding stock, they had been reintroduced in numbers late in the twenty-first century. *Here at least,* Picard thought, watching it in admiration, *is an old wrong almost put right.*

The eagle went flapping low over the col, and immediately dipped down behind it, out of sight. At the same time, something nudged Picard from behind, in the lower back. He turned to see Rollo giving him an impatient look, and eyeing his jacket pocket.

Picard lifted an amused eyebrow and produced the last piece of carrot, letting the gelding finish it. Then, "Computer," he said. "End program."

In a blink it was all gone: the wind, the burning blue, replaced by dark walls and bright gridlines burning against them. "Store program Hauts-Alpes Two-A," Picard said.

"Stored," said the computer.

Picard smiled slightly—for there was still the slightest scent of vanilla orchid in the air—and went back out of the holodeck into the real world.

Captain's log, stardate 48022.5. Pursuant to earlier orders from Starfleet Command, having relinquished the "upper" Beta Quadrant patrol run to our relief, *U.S.S. Constellation,* we have finally arrived at our designated rendezvous point near the former V843 Ophiuchi, now NGC4258.

Our new mission will involve us in several investigations which have been in progress for some time. This part of space is chiefly notable for its closeness to the Great Rift between the Sagittarius and Orion arms of the galaxy: it is a sparsely starred neighborhood, little investigated until the Federation assigned the pure science vessel *Marignano* to do a current-civilization and archaeological survey, while also examining various reported anomalies of stellar motion.

However, what should have been a quiet exploratory mission has **been** heating up somewhat. We have been reassigned to assist *Marignano,* and another starship, *Oraidhe,* has

been reassigned to this mission as well. I have
a feeling our purpose is to ride shotgun . . .
and the kind of mission which requires *two*
starships of our class to do so, this far out in
"the middle of nowhere," is one that gives me
pause . . .

Picard stood on the bridge, looking at the main
viewscreen. History lay spread out there in broad
bright streamers and clouds of hot plasma, all
burning gold and blue, the biggest bang that had
been seen in these parts for nearly twelve thousand
years.

On Earth, it was the evening of October ninth of
1604 when the astronomers of southern Europe
went out to look with great interest at an unusually
close conjunction of Jupiter and Mars. Altobelli
took himself up into the hills above Venice, Clavius
to a rise above the pines of Rome, Brunowski to the
mountains near Prague, and they all waited for
dark. It came, and Jupiter and Mars stood forth in
the sky as scheduled . . . but so did a third body,
brighter than any star or planet in the sky, swiftly
growing bright enough to be seen even in full
daylight. Clavius goggled; Altobelli stared; Brunowski ran back to his house and wrote a letter to
Johannes Kepler. Kepler studied the star nearly
nonstop until March of 1606, when it faded, and
decided it was probably the same kind of thing as
the *nova stella* or "new star" which Tycho Brahe
had described a few decades before in 1572. He

wrote a long learned paper on the *"nova"*, and the star was later often called "Kepler's star" after him. Whether he ever sent Brunowski a thank-you note, no one knows.

It was, of course, not just a common, garden variety nova, but a true supernova, only the fourth to be observed over about a thousand years, the only one to happen inside the Milky Way.

Hanging there about a light-day from the epicenter of the ancient destruction—or rather, from the point to which that center had drifted, over the course of twelve thousand years—*Enterprise* was a gilded toy, Picard reflected uneasily. He imagined how the ship must look from space, her bright side bronzed, her shadowed side sheened a deep vibrant blue by the fainter but hotter filaments of the supernova remnant, which was now flung over the equivalent of some four arc-minutes of sky, and seemed to fill everything from zenith to nadir.

"Shields holding?" Picard said softly.

"Yes, Captain," said Data, regarding the readouts on his station. "One-gigahertz flux density is holding steady at nineteen; no sign of variation from the pulsar."

"Good," Picard said. The pulsar at the center of the fragment was a "billisecond" pulsar—revolving so fast, and pulsing so swiftly, that it hardly deserved the name. Radio emissions and X rays did not propagate from it in the usual rotary pulses, but instead seemed to come blasting out in an unbroken stream, like water from a fire hose. Objects that so strenuously "pushed the envelope" of their basic definition tended to make Picard a little nervous: you never knew when they might take it on themselves to become something new and different, very abruptly, and with disastrous consequences.

"Visual on *Marignano,* Captain," Worf said.

Picard sat down. "Let's have a look."

The screen flicked to another view, fuller of blue filaments than of golden. A little gilt shape swam closer against the azure fire, decelerating from a sensible half impulse . . . for no one used warp technology while close to a supernova remnant. Until the mechanisms that had produced the remnant in the first place were better understood, stepping softly seemed wisest.

Marignano was maybe half the size of *Enterprise,* her primary hull narrower but her secondary hull as big as *Enterprise*'s and her nacelles as long. Picard remembered that the *Marignano,* like the other "long-range" science vessels, was "overengined," designed for long runs in space where there would be no repair or refit facilities except what she carried herself.

"She is hailing us, Captain," Worf said.

Picard smiled slightly. "Put her on."

The viewscreen flicked to a bridge view. Though stations were manned, the center seat was empty. The usual murmur of operations being handled could be heard, but over it all, a lively, slightly raspy voice was saying, "—on, I want that report. It should have been here five minutes ago."

The voice's owner leaned into pickup for the viewscreen. "Hello, Jean-Luc!"

Picard smiled. It was always that way with her: you might not have seen Ileen Maisel for five years, or ten, but she would infallibly pick up the conversation in a tone of voice that suggested you had last spoken about a day ago.

"Hello, Ileen," he said, wondering, as he looked at her, whether those roving tendencies of hers, and the matching tendencies of mind, were what kept her looking so young. She looked much as she had when their paths last crossed, five years ago, a woman of medium height, slender but with a sturdy look about her. Tightly curled, shortish salt-and-pepper hair, heavier on the pepper than the salt. Vivid blue-gray eyes and a big cheerful grin, a mobile, expressive face. That was Ileen—that, and a powerfully projected sense of purpose and speed: she had things to do, and was not going to let the universe hold her up.

"You're late," she said, plopping herself down in her center chair and stealing a peek at the padd she was holding. "I thought you were going to be here seventeen standard hours ago."

Picard cleared his throat and shot a somewhat concealed look of amusement at Riker, who simply blinked, refusing to rise to the bait. The rendezvous, as was usual procedure when such huge distances were involved, had not been set for a specific time, but for a "rendezvous envelope" between a given stardate and another. "That was the *earliest* we could have made it," Picard said. "And doubtless you *were* here early, the way you go charging around the place. Have you heard anything from *Oraidhe?*"

"Not a squeak since day before yesterday, but we've still got a day's worth of envelope," Captain Maisel said. "I swear, Clif would be late for his own funeral."

"Exaggeration," Picard said gently. "But Starfleet was a little elliptical about the details of this mission, and I take it you want us to get on with something urgent."

"Everything is urgent," Ileen said, giving Picard a look that suggested she was astonished to have to tell him so. "But, yeah, there are some sensitive aspects to this, and the sooner we're on our way, the better."

"You wouldn't consider giving us a little jump on the mission briefing, would you, Captain?" Riker said.

"What, before Clif gets here?" Maisel said. "That would be most improper, Commander. Is dinner included in that offer?"

Riker chuckled; this time it was he who gave Picard the sidelong glance. Picard, straightfaced, said, "I wouldn't like to make you work on an empty stomach, Ileen. Shall we say two hours from now?"

"You're on," she said. "I want to do a little polishing on my data, anyway. Later—"

And she was gone, leaving them looking once more at the torn golden veils of Kepler's Star, and at *Marignano,* settling in to station-keep beside them.

"Social, isn't she?" Riker said.

"In passing, absolutely," Picard said, getting up again. "But her heart is out in the empty places; even *this* far out is too far in for her, I think. In the old days on *Pathfinder,* she used to complain that we 'never got out of Earth's backyard.'"

"Not a problem she has now, I take it."

Picard shook his head. "Not at all. Well, I confess I'm curious to hear the specifics of this operation. Starfleet said little more than that it might be long-term: we're to evaluate and decide how best to cooperate with *Marignano* when the situation becomes clear."

"I'll have a buffet set up in one of the briefing rooms," Riker said, getting up to go see to it.

There was a soft chirp from one of the panels. Worf listened briefly, then said, "Captain, *Oraidhe* has just come out of warp on the other side of Kepler's Star. Captain Clif has sent a greeting and says he will be available to meet with you, and they will be here in about ninety minutes."

Picard nodded. "Acknowledge the message with thanks."

The captain turned toward his first officer.

"Go on, Number One; roll out the red carpet.

Both these ships have come a long way, and we have a reputation for hospitality to maintain . . ."

Two hours later, the red carpet was out with a vengeance. The briefing room was full of department heads and bridge staff, a tidy buffet, and a slightly unusual feature: three captains.

Picard invited his bridge crew and senior officers to attend, mostly for social purposes. The serious briefing would not be until the next afternoon—all three ships were taking a day to rotate their senior crew onto alpha shift, for convenience's sake.

Ileen Maisel had come over with her bridge crew, including another officer Picard knew, Storennan Grace, a short, stony-skinned Centaurrin who had also been on *Stargazer* with them. She introduced her science officer, a cheerful young woman named Frances Pickup, and her exec, tall, lanky Paul McGrady. As always seemed to happen at these occasions, some of Ileen's crew turned out to know some of the *Enterprise* people: Pickup turned out to have taken some classes with Troi, years before, and another of Ileen's people, her senior conn officer Kil Colgan, had once had a broken arm set by Dr. Crusher.

Then, a little later, in the midst of a welter of "Do you knows" and "Have you seens," in came Captain Gohod Clif. Picard stood to greet him, very glad indeed to meet him physically at last; he knew him from reputation, and from the occasional conversation when the paths of their starships had crossed during missions. Clif shook Picard's hand cordially. He was a big, tall, handsome man, broad across the shoulders and fair-complected, the characteristic skin dappling of a Trill host paler on him than usual, vanishing up into a shock of silver-blond hair.

"It's been a year or two, hasn't it?" said Picard. "During our last refit."

"That's right: I was in for a yearly debriefing." Clif's voice was big, to match the rest of him. "After that, they sent me over to Eleven Lacerti, that civil war . . . then the usual patrol duty. I was glad to come out this way. Looks like things are quieter."

Ileen, who had wandered over to join them, looked at Clif with an amused expression. "I wouldn't bet on it," she said. "You wouldn't be here otherwise. But we'll be getting to that. Lobster, Clif?"

Clif introduced his science officer, Tamastara, a handsome slender Orynchid lady completely covered in soft gray fur; and his exec, Elen Miraitis, an Andorian. They got talking to the *Enterprise* and *Marignano* crew members, and the three captains took themselves off to one side of the room to eat and small-talk for a while. Picard mentioned Pentarus V, and the events surrounding the *Phoenix* incident on the borders of Cardassian space, and was privately glad that Wolf 359 was now far enough in the past not to come up automatically as a topic of conversation. Clif had been nearly at the other side of Federation space for half the year, and had spent three of the last six months getting back to "inner" space, before being sent off out this way a month previously to meet *Marignano*. He and Picard amused themselves for a couple of minutes playing an informal version of the "who's been out farthest" game, as if they were a couple of Earth-born cadets bragging about who'd first been to the moon. Ileen watched them with a tolerant smile while they calculated light-years and parsecs in their heads. Clif won by a hair, AX Arae being a bare twelve parsecs farther than 1020 Octantis, Picard's farthest distance reached by normal means. He stopped himself just short of mention-ing extragalactic distances. *Those were accidental,* he thought wryly, *and it doesn't seem fair to brag . . .*

"And you, Ileen," Clif said. "I saw you last—where?"

"It's got to be sixteen years ago now," she said, sitting down again; she had been up getting another glass of wine. "I was sorry to hear about Rael, by the way."

Clif nodded, looking just a touch sad. "I got your note. It was much appreciated." He paused for a moment, then smiled, only half-convincingly, as he did a brisk search for a less painful topic. "Well, you've certainly taken the grand tour since then."

"Yes," she said. "A long time out here at the empty end of things. About two years, alone, on this segment of the investigative sequence." She waved at the map showing on the screen, on which *Marignano*'s course for the last few standard years was plotted: a long, leisurely, waving line, wandering through the huge volume of space at the fringes of the Sagittarius Arm. Picard, used to much less casual and easygoing course sequences, looked at it with mild envy.

"That's an investigative sequence?" Clif said, bemused. "It looks more like an inebriated stagger."

Ileen laughed. "You spent too long running the inner-system routes, Clif; you're too used to straight lines. We just slouch along looking at stars and planets and nebulae and things, checking to see if there's anything interesting that no one else has seen; and if one of the science staff convinces me that we need to go back the way we came, we do it."

"Nice work if you can get it," said Picard, with a wry smile.

She leaned back in her seat, crossing her legs comfortably. "It is," Maisel said.

She reached out to get a cracker from a nearby tray. "Now, while we're doing our long-term studies, there's plenty of opportunity to look into other matters in this neighborhood as well. This might be a fairly empty part of space nowadays, but it wasn't once, as I think you both have heard."

Picard nodded; this lay within his area of expertise. "I haven't looked into it in all that much detail," Picard said, "but there are supposed to be a surprising number of so-called vacated planets around here. Worlds that were inhabited once, by sentient species, but which those species seem to have simply moved away from."

"Or died out," Clif said. "Sometimes under odd circumstances. Species that otherwise seemed perfectly robust, civilizations that were peaceful, or at least stable . . . just gone, suddenly. Not overnight, but too quickly, in light of what records or other traces they might have left."

"The so-called planetary *Marie Celeste* phenomenon," Picard said. It was a proposition that had haunted his dreams, some nights. *How does a whole civilization just disappear like that? One ship, five ships or ten, in the dangerous vastness of space, yes. But whole worlds . . . ?*

Ileen nodded, looking a touch cranky, as if the vanished planets were a personal affront. "That's right. Well, all we've had to go on, until we started these surveys five years ago, were rumors about a lot of these species. Now, slowly, we're beginning to amass some data, as we've started to work on the archaeological side of our studies." She looked sideways at Picard, grinning, as he suddenly straightened in his seat. "Yes, I *thought* that would get your attention. Some of these 'missing' or vacated worlds turn out, after all, to have suffered the planetary equivalent of 'natural deaths.' You remember all those rumors about the Disarrui?"

"A little 'pocket empire,'" Picard said, nodding; he had done some research into them, a couple of years back. "They were based around Eighteen Sixty-five Serpens, I think. Star-capable, and very active traders, a couple of thousand years ago—"

"That's right," Ileen said. "And then all of a sudden, *poof!* They were gone, no one could figure out where. Well, the *poof* was real enough, as it turns out, but rumors of something suspicious about their demise turn out to have been exaggerated. We managed to track down the original Disarrui home system—it was one of those that suffered from abnormal drift, and that drift, unfortunately, took them into the path of a large gravitationally affiliated association of post-planetary-formation debris."

"A meteor," Picard said immediately, horror and interest intermingled. "A big one."

"About the size of Earth's moon," Ileen said, "if the fracture signatures in the planet's remains are to be trusted, and I think they are—there was almost no time for tidal effects. Well, the planet was completely destroyed. The ancillary planets in nearby systems weren't harmed; but unfortunately the Disarrui, as far as we can tell from records left in those systems, were one of those species who have a 'geobond' to the homeworld, an empathic or maybe telepathic connection to the physical structure of the planet itself. When their homeworld was destroyed, the Disarrui couldn't survive the blow; they all died as well—just withered away over the course of a century or two. Their remaining worlds have been pretty conclusively plundered, over time, but there were enough clues to make clear what happened."

Picard shook his head sadly. "Grave robbers," he murmured, frowning.

"There's a lot of that up here," Ileen said. "But still, not as much as you might think. The area has a reputation, it seems, for being a little strange. Those 'vanished worlds'—" She made a vague, "disappearing" gesture with her fingers. "No one knew quite what to make of them, even a couple hundred years ago. No one who was routinely in this part of space had drift analysis technology that was advanced enough to predict correctly where things had gone. So legends started springing up. Old lost races, hiding their whole star systems from the curious or the rapacious. Incredibly rich species, incredibly wise ones. Sometimes, incredibly dangerous ones . . . species whose worlds it was literally death to find. There was never any evidence for most of these . . . but the legends linger."

"I suppose," Clif said, leaning back in his chair and stretching, "you have to explain mysterious losses somehow. Who really enjoys acknowledging accident, or stupidity, for what they are?"

"Still," Picard said, "among a great number of species—our own included—there's a delight in mystery, in the unexplained that lurks out past the edges of the maps."

"True enough," Ileen said.

Clif looked thoughtful as he sipped his own wine. "Ah, but mystery is so often accompanied by danger. Without any major force present to provide protection," he said, "such scattered settlements, strewn over hundreds of light-years and far away from the normal trade lanes, can't be very safe."

"They're not," Ileen said. "There's piracy out this way, a fair amount of it. Not just raiders who come looking for undefended newly settled planets, or lightly armed colony ships in transit, but more of your grave robbers, Jean-Luc—all kinds of opportunists, drawn by all these sketchy legends of vacated planets left full of ancient treasures ripe for the looting. So—" Ileen stretched, smiled. "To 'pull our weight,' *Marignano* does a fair amount of convoy work in this sector—escorting trading ships coming through, colony vessels, you name it."

"Must be interesting," Clif said.

Ileen gave him a look suggesting what he could do with his definition of *interesting*. "I can't tell you how many times I've had to break off a line of investigation into something *really* interesting to go escort some goddamn warp-driven shopping center. That's why our course keeps sprouting those little curly bits, here and there." She waved at the screen. "However, doing that work enables me to do my *real* work, so I'm satisfied."

"I take it, though," said Picard, "that things have been getting too hot for a pure science vessel's armaments to handle."

Ileen looked rueful. "Afraid so. We've been here

long enough to make some judgments about how many ships 'ought' to go missing in a given period. A baseline estimate, anyway. Well, over the past year I've been noticing that baseline edging up a little, and then over the last three months, we lost three ships, two merchants and a colonization vessel, bang, bang, bang, one after the other. That made me twitchy, and I had words with Starfleet about it. Too many ships were becoming statistics . . . and I'd sooner we didn't become one, too. Something else started, though, which may have tipped them over the edge as regards doing something—though I would have thought the ship disappearances would have been enough. I mentioned that there's a fair amount of archaeological work going on out this way. There are usually about ten digs going on at any one time, and keeping an eye on them all has always been difficult. Well, in the past six months, four digs, all very remote from one another, have been attacked and plundered. Sometimes with loss of life: the dig at Sixteen-sixteen Ophiuchi Six was not only stripped bare, but the raiders killed Saeo Uristilaen."

"Heavens about us," Clif said softly.

"Ileen, I hadn't heard," Picard said softly. "And after all that groundbreaking work on the Infarret . . ."

"He'll never finish it now," Ileen said sadly.

"Do they have any idea who did this?"

"We. No. We got the distress call from the survivors, all right, but by the time we got there, the trail was cold. Ion-trail residues in the area had been wiped out by the local solar wind—the damn star's too active for its own good anyway, which may have also been the reason why the Infarret aren't still around. We did some cursory searching, but we knew it would do no good, and finally, so did Starfleet. I just wish they would have realized this increase of local piracy was a problem before Uristilaen had to convince them of it by dying."

The three captains looked grimly at one another. *All of us,* Picard thought, *have been in situations where we warned Starfleet that something bad was about to happen, and they wouldn't believe us until it did, and then it was too late, the damage done.*

"So," Ileen said. "We have to finish the investigation surrounding the Infarret dig. It'll take a while to get over there from way over here, of course. But meantime, we three ships are to begin aggressively patrolling this sector of space, visiting all local digs and making it plain to anyone out there who's watching that the level of protection has been stepped up considerably. Starfleet puts a lot of credence in the idea that the simple added presence of your two ships here will cut in on the number of attacks on both archaeological digs and transient ships."

Clif nodded. "We'll be patrolling together at first?"

"For a good while," Ileen said. "The sight of our three ships in company will give people pause, it's true . . . but it'll also give them the sense that we're more likely to be found together than apart, so that when we do split up, later in the mission, our adversaries out there will never be too sure that the other two ships aren't somewhere nearby. That'll work to our advantage."

"Except," Clif said, rather wryly, "when they're not . . . and someone pushes the issue."

Ileen shrugged. "I've been pushing back alone for a while now, and I don't have half the armament you two do. You'll do all right, I think. The main advantage we have here is that the raiders seem to travel alone, or only in very small groups. They don't trust one another; that's good for us."

"Not much of an advantage," Picard said, "but it'll do. So do you have a schedule set up for us yet?"

"A tentative one. That's going to your execs as well. Look it over and see how you like it. I've targeted some areas for special attention, places where we've had trouble before and I'd like to make a show of strength. Anyplace else that attracts your attention, for whatever reason, let me know and I'll make whatever changes you require."

Picard and Clif nodded. "Great," Ileen said. "Excuse me, gentlemen; I'm going to go do some justice to this spread."

She headed for the buffet table with an expression of great intensity. Picard watched her go with amusement, and found Clif looking first at her, then at him. "You've known each other for a while?" he said.

Picard nodded. "About twenty years, on and off," he said.

Clif shook his head, laughing softly. "I don't know her that well myself, but I think I know her well enough to suspect that she's spoiling for a fight."

"I'd say you were right," Picard said. "Specifically, I suspect she's had to be careful and circumspect for a long time, out here all by herself . . . and I suspect she's hated it."

"Well," Clif said, "I've been in the same position, on and off. Little commands, out in the middle of nowhere, no one to back you up . . . and then you suddenly get your wish: a big ship, lots of weaponry . . ."

"And typically," Picard said, "the threats you would have loved to use all that hardware on dry up completely."

Clif put up an eyebrow. "This far out," he said, "I would hope you're right. If trouble does arise, I would prefer it would be the kind that three ships can handle easily."

Picard nodded, thinking—as he had been for some time—that any kind of problem that Starfleet thought *needed* three ships as heavily armed as they all were was one he personally could do without. But duty gave you no chance to refuse; and truth to tell, even with the danger, to be out in an area of space so little known and surveyed, in which so much knowledge and history lay buried, he felt he could live with the risk.

"It won't be all trouble, of course," Clif said. "On missions like this, one always underestimates the boredom factor early on . . . and then, much later, you find yourself wishing for the trouble."

"Not me, Captain," Picard said, wry. "But you'll have known a lot more boredom in your time than I will have."

Clif nodded and smiled wearily. "Two hundred years now," he said, "here and there: first in the Trill private service, then in Starfleet when we joined. But I think we'll have a lot less boredom on this run. We're a long way from help, should we stumble across anything that suggests that even *we* have to call for backup. I've been here before . . . and this space can be full of surprises."

Picard reached for the wine bottle, raised his eyebrows. Clif nodded. "Tell me," said Picard. "And don't confine yourself to the neighborhood. Two hundred years must produce some stories worth hearing."

Clif smiled.

Chapter Two

THE NEXT DAY they pulled away from Kepler's Star, three ships in company. Picard sat in his command chair holding himself still, mostly because his sides still hurt from laughing at some of Clif's more outrageous stories from the night before.

With great purpose he turned his attention to Riker. "The course," Riker was saying to Troi, sitting as usual at Picard's left hand, "is a little weird . . . another version of what Captain Clif described as an 'inebriated stagger.' It's meant to give the various raiders in this area the idea that we might turn up anywhere."

"It certainly gives *me* that idea," Troi said. She was eyeing one of the side screens, where the course was displaying. "A lot of dashing around in the early stages, anyway." Data turned toward the counselor with a quizzical expression on his pale golden face. Troi smiled. "Did you want to add something, Data?"

"If I might point out, Counselor," Data said. "The course still serves our mission, both the escort-and-convoy segment and the continuation of Captain Maisel's galactic drift survey. It is also incidentally statistically satisfying in terms of seeking out new loci of untoward occurrence—"

Picard blinked at that, and Riker, too, looked bemused. "Excuse me, Mr. Data. I passed my statistics courses without too much trouble, but what the devil is a 'locus of untoward occurrence'?"

"It is an area, either experiential or physical, in which a significant percentage of undesirable conditions obtain," said Data. "These include a wide range of objective and subjective phenomena, including structural and ethical failures—"

Troi began to smile again. "'Ethical failures'? Data, are you implying that the structure of space understands ethics?"

If he didn't know better, Picard would have sworn that the android looked confused. "The theoretical terminology employed simply refers to various scholia of mathematics which contain ethical modes, such as Trill and Hamalki. 'Ethics' in mathematics merely refers to those ranges of physical results deemed undesirable, a highly subjective and variable subset—"

Oh, dear, Picard thought, *here we go . . .*

"Wait a minute," Riker said. "It looks like we've come right around in a circle here. Mr. Data, let me hazard a guess. Are you saying that this course has a better than even chance of taking us somewhere where something 'bad' will happen? A raid on a world where there's an archaeological dig going on, or an attack on a settled planet or a ship in transit? Something of that kind?"

"Yes, Commander," Data said. "The mathematics involved are grounded in a variant of lottery theory. Taking into account more recent developments in statistical technique, such as those reservoir description and stochastic modeling theorems advanced over the past several decades by T'Veih and Oronal, it is obvious that—"

Picard raised an eyebrow and once again began studying the padd he was holding. What he had learned some time back was that when Mr. Data uttered the words "It is obvious that . . . ," it was sometimes better for one's temper to start getting caught up on the paperwork. He stayed where he was, though, watching as Troi began to find the bridge ceiling unusually interesting.

"—an extension of so-called fourth-order Venn-atypical locus variant identifications," Data went on, oblivious, "can be expanded to include specific occurrences in space-time, including the occurrences of high-ion-flux patches such as remain in—for example—the wake of armed engagements in or out of warp, each kind of residue generating its own residue which a sufficiently complex equation may include and predict. Within normal statistical parameters, of course."

"Of course," Riker said, his blue eyes glittering with glee. He glanced at Troi, who was trying mightily to suppress a yawn. Perhaps it was time for the captain to step in and rescue his beleaguered crew, thought Picard.

"Such kinds of analysis have been bruited about for a while," the captain said. "Some Starfleet statisticians were suggesting that all Starfleet ships should routinely follow such 'negative-satisfaction' courses. The idea didn't last long. What serving captain would sit still for being forced into patrols where the chance of something *good* happening was purposely minimized?" He smiled a little grimly, remembering the uproar at one captains' conference where the issue had been discussed. "And the chair warmers who came up with the idea very quickly forgot it and came up with something else less controversial."

"Well. It seems to me," Riker said, stretching in his chair and folding his arms as if settling in to really get his teeth into this idea, "that it ought to be equally possible to design courses that would sort for loci of 'toward' occurrences. Wouldn't it, Data? If this scholium of mathematics were reliable enough, you ought to be able to work out courses on which nothing but *good* things would happen."

"The question would remain," Troi said, looking mischievous now, "good for *whom?* Surely that needs another value judgment."

"Well, for example, for the starship personnel."

"Sir," Data said, looking grave. "The variables are at present so many, and handling them so complex, that it would take years of analysis to determine such courses reliably. But bearing in mind a Starfleet ship's basic brief—among other things, to assist vessels in distress—pursuing those courses would not be ethical."

"Isn't this where I came in?" said Riker. He stretched again, with a slight sound of joints popping, then got up, grimacing.

The wince made Picard put his eyebrows up, slightly surprised. "Physical problems, Number One?"

"Nothing serious, Captain. Dr. Crusher said I needed to get a little extra exercise this week, so Mr. Worf very . . . kindly programmed a Klingon workout into the holodeck for me." Riker grimaced again. "Klingon exercise trainers are, uh, enthusiastic."

Worf, behind his console, smiled very slightly and said nothing. Then he glanced down, and his face changed. "Captain—"

Picard glanced up. "Mr. Worf?"

"Radiation readings, sir," Worf said, touching his console here and there. "The space we are presently transiting is 'hotter' than I expected."

At that, Picard looked thoughtfully at Data, who had already begun consulting his own console. Data said, "Background temperature of the interstellar medium is elevated by the adjusted equivalent of two degrees Kelvin, a fairly significant rise over what would normally be considered normal."

"Causes?"

Worf was still studying his panel with increasing interest, Picard noted. "Particle decay residues in this area contain exotics," Worf said. "Lacking an astronomical cause—"

Data's hands were dancing over his console now, but after a moment he shook his head. "We are sufficiently far from Kepler's Star now to discount any effect from the supernova remnant," he said, "and surrounding stars show no overt signs of flares or other abnormality. Additionally, flares only rarely cause such high percentages of exotics."

"Then these readings could be considered evidence of a battle of some kind in this area," Worf said, "with considerable use of phasers or other energy weapons."

Picard smiled a small, grim smile. "Abstruse mathematics aside," he said, "if you go looking for trouble, you'll find it:—and we came looking. Mr. Worf, call *Oraidhe* and *Marignano.*"

"*Oraidhe* is hailing us, Captain."

"Put them on."

Oraidhe's bridge showed itself on the viewscreen, with Captain Clif standing behind his center chair, looking over his shoulder at his own security officer's panel. "Captain, there seems to have been some kind of fracas in this area recently."

"We think so, too," Picard said.

"Sir," Data said, "if I read these data correctly, I would suggest that there were two main groups or forces. One was significantly larger than the other, and it, or elements of it, headed off to the galactic northward after the engagement, if, as I judge, a running engagement was indeed the source of these readings."

"The trail looks fairly cold, though," said Clif. "Captain, we'll shoot our projections over to you and to *Marignano*. I would hope Mr. Data would lend us his assistance in this regard."

"The trail proper is at approximately four degrees K, which is cold by most standards," Data said.

Oraidhe's science officer, who was standing behind the captain, nodded her head in Data's direction. "All the meson residues out there are showing signs of decay, but not of stripping," she said. "We're going to have to do some pretty aggressive scanning before we go much further."

"Let's do it then," Picard said. "Captain?"

"Our preparation for continuous-stream link are just about complete," Clif said. "We may as well finish the tests on the system now, and see how well it actually works."

He nodded to his science officer, grinned a little at Picard. "We'll be in touch."

The screen flickered. Another voice said, "Hey, Jean-Luc, the game's afoot!"

"So I see, Ileen," he said. *"Oraidhe* will be activating data stream momentarily. Are you ready to link in?"

"Are we ready?" she said, sounding amused and annoyed. "For two weeks now. What else do you think we did while we were waiting for you two to show up? Come on, time's a-wasting."

"Ready for data-stream link," Mr. Worf said. "Set for terabaud bandwidth during evaluation."

"Initiate."

Nothing happened, but then Picard didn't expect anything to, at least not for a while. Not for a long while.

On and off for the next three days, Picard watched Data sifting information about decay traces through his computers, like someone slowly, patiently panning for gold, hunting that one flake, one grain, that will tell him whether he's wasting his time. Almost every time the captain came on the bridge, he found Data talking to either Tamastara on *Oraidhe* or Ileen's enthusiastic science officer Pickup on *Marignano*. But after a while, Tamastara's even calm appeared to be acquiring an edge to it, while Pickup's enthusiasm seemed to be getting some of its edges worn off.

Though Picard understood the need for slow, careful research as well as anyone else, this kind of work he found as wearing to watch as it must be for the people working on it; so he stayed out of the way, and busied himself with the hundred other things that required daily attention on a ship the *Enterprise*'s size.

On the fourth day of this, though, when Picard came onto the bridge for a look around, preparatory to going off shift, Data looked up at him. The front viewscreen was split between views of *Marignano*'s science station and *Oraidhe*'s, and the two other science officers were there, looking worn-out but very pleased. "Captain," Data said, "I believe we have a result."

He glanced at the other two science officers; both of them shook their heads. "Mr. Data did most of it," Tamastara said mildly.

Picard nodded. "Mr. Data?"

"Captain, we have a very faint trace leading off in the direction of chi Scorpii. A slight predominance of rho-mesons in the space in that direction over the past several hours. It appears to be getting stronger."

"How close is our quarry, then?"

"The vessel responsible for these decays is no closer than five light-years and no farther than fifty," Data said. "I cannot provide a closer reading until we have followed this trail long enough to better judge the speed at which the trace becomes more concentrated. I would estimate, however, that the ship that left it is not one ship, but several moving in company."

"And we're all agreed," Tamastara said, "that the ship leaving the telltale is one of Federation or

Fed-allied make and build, one of the Ilenya types, mark eight to twelve."

"We'd better go after that trail, then," said Picard.

Over the next day, the concentration and energy spent by the crew involved in the chase gave Picard a whole new set of referents for the word *tension*. Data never left his post, and his concentration mostly reminded Picard of a holodeck Holmes, hot on the trail of one of Moriarty's more nefarious schemes. From the main screen, at any given moment, when Picard looked out of the ready room, he might find Tamastara or Pickup looking over at Data as they worked together, both wearing the same kind of rapt and hungry look as hunters after some quarry. Picard had to force himself to stay off of the bridge.

There was a flurry of excitement that brought him in, late in the afternoon: the sudden discovery, not only of an increased number of particles in the local space, but of scrap—metal and plastic fragments, and plasma residues which indicated that here their quarry had been brought to battle.

"It was not a long engagement, Captain," Data said, with Worf looking over his shoulder at his readings. "But a large number of vessels were indeed involved—and it is difficult to say exactly how many without knowing their sizes, and the residues do not allow such close analysis."

"And you have a clear trail from here?"

"One trail is very strong, compared to what we were following when we began. The other is tenuous, while indicating low warp capacity."

Worf eyed the heads-up display on the main viewscreen. "The first trail will bring us to the victors."

"So it will," Picard said. "Yellow alert, then, while we pursue."

And the pursuit went on, for hours, and hours more. Picard finally went to his quarters. It was during one of the dog watches, when Picard was still too tense to read and too tense to sleep that his commbadge went off.

"Picard!" he barked, rather more loudly than he had intended to.

"Captain," Data's voice said, "we have instrument readings on our quarry. Thirty-five light-years out."

"What is it?"

"ID is uncertain as yet. Six ships, traveling together: three large, three small. That is all we can tell just now."

"Very well," Picard said. "I'm on my way."

When he got there, Picard looked around the bridge, thoughtful. It was only mildly unusual that Riker was there. Will had changed his active shift to pick up where Picard's had left off for the duration of the chase. Finding Worf there as well was equally unusual, but then again, it was all too like him anyway to volunteer for extra duty; many Klingons got as much energy from extra work as humans got from resting. Troi was there as well, though looking a little hollow-eyed. She just barely kept from stifling a yawn as Picard came in.

"Counselor?" he said, sitting down beside her.

"Excitement," she said, glancing around her at the others, "can be difficult to shut out sometimes. I gave up trying."

The screen ahead showed the several tiny sparks of light that *Enterprise* and her sisters had been chasing all this while. "Warp signatures coming up now, Captain," Data said. "Federation technology." The android turned toward Picard. "These would appear to be Lalairu ships."

Picard nodded, sitting back in his chair with a slight sigh. That took a load off his mind. The Lalairu traded wherever they went . . . and they went everywhere. Finding them here was less of a surprise than finding anyone else, though even for them, in these debatable spaces, the trading opportunities might seem to be somewhat limited. No matter—if there were any opportunities, the Lalairu would find them.

"The commander of the lead vessel is asking to speak to you privately, Captain," said Mr Worf.

"Very well," Picard said. "I'll take it in my ready room."

He sat down behind his desk and touched his screen. It came alive to show a bridge so dimly lit it was almost impossible to see. A shape moved out of the shadows, forward to the screen. It was very tall, slender, and pale, and had a humanoid form. Picard peered at it, and then realized he was seeing what few people had, a Lalairu without the protective, self-grown "cloak" it wore outside its own ship and shed again when it came home.

"Captain Picard," said the Lalairu, "I greet you. I am called Elekk."

"I am pleased to make your acquaintance, Elekk."

Elekk bowed at the courtesy. "You are very welcome to these spaces, Captain. The leader of our leaders of families has mentioned that she heard you were coming this way, and she instructed us to help you in whatever way we can. Not that we would not have done so in any case. What brings you to this part of the worlds?"

Once again it became plain to Picard that the only thing to travel faster than starships was news, and he wondered who at Starfleet had decided to help him out by putting a word in a trustworthy ear. "We were following the traces of a battle which seems to have taken place some thirty or more light-years from here," Picard said, "and in which you seem to have been involved."

Elekk laughed, a soft hissing sound. "We were indeed, Captain. All others involved in the attack except for two ships, we think, have predeceased us."

Picard's mouth quirked at the terminology. Lalairu counted an existence's experience by how often one died, and their definition of death was one they found difficult to explain to other species: some form of regeneration often seemed to be involved. There had been problems about this until the Lalairu had been made to understand that in other species, death was almost always permanent.

"Well," Picard said, "perhaps you'll help us unravel this business. Who exactly were your attackers?"

"They were *athwaen,*" the Lalairu said. "I think your word is *pirates.* They came up with us at—" Elekk paused, studied the panel in front of him. "These coordinates, which I shall pass to you—and began firing. They were a force of approximately fifteen vessels; one large one of approximately light-cruiser size, and various others down to corvette size or smaller."

"Did they communicate with you at all first?"

Elekk laughed softly, another hiss, with more of an edge to it. "No, they fired first; so we defended ourselves."

"Against *fifteen* vessels—" Picard said, raising an eyebrow.

Elekk looked back at him. "Our armaments are something out of the ordinary. We spend a lot of our time out in the emptier spaces, far from other species' protection . . . so we make sure we can protect ourselves. We are in the process of preparing a report on this incident. If it would help you, Captain Picard, we will gladly make available to you our recordings of the battle, and all associated data."

"Please do," Picard said. "Meantime, what came of the attack?"

Elekk folded himself down onto the large comfortable-looking sofa that seemed to serve as command chair. "Fourteen of the vessels we destroyed. One we could not account for—I think you would say it got lost in the shuffle. The largest one escaped. It was still warp-capable at low speeds, but had very little weapons capacity left to it."

"Which way did they go?"

"To the galactic north," said Elekk. "I would suspect that if you hurry, you can catch them . . . assuming you are interested in doing so."

"Certainly. We would not care for those who commit piracy to be encouraged in the belief that it can be committed with impunity."

"And when you catch them?"

Picard thought about that. "Well, naturally we would attempt to get them to surrender, board and secure their ship, and send them off with one of our task force to a starbase."

"Captain," Elekk said, "if I were in your position, I would blow them up and be done with them."

Picard paused. "That is not a course Starfleet would approve our pursuing."

The Lalairu nodded. "I know. But I fear that the beings involved in this kind of endeavor understand mercy as weakness. And they understand death as well."

"With due respect," Picard said, "death is not an unfamiliar concept to the Lalairu, either."

"Captain, you're quite right," Elekk said. "But our people, who can regenerate a whole body from a fragment, or even from a coil of DNA, see death as just another kind of life experience. For other species . . ." The Lalairu looked thoughtful. "Well, I must say it took us a while to understand how you manage to die and not come back. But when we did understand that, we took to killing your kind with more restraint . . . to act otherwise would have been unacceptable."

Picard smiled slightly, amused. Unacceptable indeed.

"Captain," Elekk said, "perhaps, also with respect, I might say that Earth humans have a gift for prolonging their own problems. I hope that these pirates may, when you catch up with them, give you an opportunity to exercise your version of right behavior. My guess is that they will not; and I urge you to look to your shields."

"Elekk," Picard said, "thank you for the warning. If you'll send those data on your attack over to us for analysis, we'd be grateful. Meanwhile, is there anything that we can assist you with?"

The Lalairu looked thoughtful, if Picard was reading his expression correctly. "Perhaps your quartermaster's department and ours could exchange 'want lists.'"

"Let's do that, and travel in company for a little

while until the details have been sorted out. My executive officer will see to it."

"Until we meet again, then, Captain," said Elekk. "In more pleasant circumstances, I hope." The screen flickered off.

Picard went back out to the bridge and had just started to instruct Riker in what needed to be done when Worf interrupted. "Captain," the Klingon said, "the Lalairu ship is hailing us again."

"On screen."

"Captain," said Elekk as the screen flicked back into image again. "I do beg your pardon. I neglected to mention that about a hundred hours ago we had an encounter with a colony craft transiting this area; a ship called *Boreal.*"

Picard thought back. "Yes," he said. "The name's on our list of vessels in transit through this area." It was a privately owned ship, one that contracted its services out to do colonial relocations and supply work. "Was it having any problems?"

"Ah," said the Lalairu. "Well. It reported no malfunctions or difficulties. But they were rather . . . cavalier about their communications techniques."

"In what way?"

"Well, they *did* appear to be using phasers for them. They shot at us before we could identify ourselves to them."

"And you—"

"Did *not* fire back at them, Captain." This time there was no mistaking the amused look. "We identified ourselves and passed on . . . but they were rather rude to us. They seemed to mistake us for a Federation ship, or one in the employ of the Federation."

"That would be a serious error," said Picard. If there was anything the Lalairu valued, it was their nonaligned status: their strict neutrality kept them safe in spaces where anyone else would come to grief . . . although it had occurred to Picard several times that their neutrality was much enhanced by their heavy armaments. Lalairu weapons gave third parties second thoughts.

"At any rate, Captain, they reported all well, and continued on their way, heading for One Twenty-seven Scorpii, I believe. But it might be wise to warn other ships in the area."

"We'll look into it. And good luck on the rest of your journey."

"Any journey is good, Captain," said the Lalairu, genuinely smiling now. "Whether it goes well or ill depends on the company. May yours go well also." The screen winked out.

Picard looked up at Riker, who was returning to his seat. "Would you say that Mr. Data's problematic course is working yet?" he said.

"Hard to tell, Captain," said Riker. "I prefer a slightly larger universe of statistical data, myself."

"There are some new data available now, Commander," Data said. "We have received the transmission of the records of the Lalairu engagement with the raiders."

"Put it on the screen in my ready room, Mr. Data," said Picard. "Number One, let's have a look."

It was interesting material, and rather distressing. The transmission began with an image of the Lalairu ships sailing along, about their lawful business. In the background, far away, Kepler's Star shone, still—even at this distance—the brightest thing to be seen in circumambient space. Then, suddenly, fire in the night, as all around the Lalairu convoy, the sixteen pirate ships—mostly long needlelike shapes, compared to the generally rounded, fat-bodied little Lalairu craft—came out of warp in two loosely arranged hemispheres and closed on the Lalairu in a pincers movement.

Picard's mouth tightened to a straight line as he watched. It was a standard enough englobement, the movement designed to take an enemy swiftly by surprise and overload his weapons computers before he had a chance to respond.

This group of Lalairu were certainly experts. Picard barely had time to draw breath between the appearance of the englobing pirate vessels and the equally sudden appearance of the lines of light that stabbed out from the Lalairu ships. In that initial onslaught, targeting with astonishing precision—bearing in mind the suddenness of the attack—

some five of the pirate vessels were destroyed, all making a gap toward one side of the globe formation. And a second after that, a network of tractor beams leaped out from one to another of the Lalairu vessels, welding them together for the moment in one single structure, pulling them close together.

For a moment Picard thought that the structure would fail, that the ships would crash into one another. But with barely a kilometer's space left among them, the little tight-packed aggregate of ships sprouted a common warp field and, at low but precisely angled warp, shot out of the englobement.

"They've done this before," Riker said softly. Picard nodded. Only a tenth of a second's warp was needed to get them free of the globe. Then the tractors dropped away; each Lalairu ship went into warp independently, spreading out and around the pirate ships . . . and suddenly the englobers were the englobed.

Then the phaser fire and the photon torpedoes lanced out in earnest. The earlier display had been merely a flourish of weapons, the unsheathing of the sword. Now the sword smote. One after another, the pirate vessels' shields went down, and as they went down, they were destroyed.

One after another, the pirate ships flared into vapor, were gone. Picard saw one go arcing away into the night, leaking gases in long, glittering, crystallizing plumes. The second one, the light-cruiser-sized vessel, fought a while more, but eventually it, too, limped away; and the Lalairu, having been unable to destroy it, let it go and resumed the original course.

There the record ended, except for details of the Lalairu damage control operation: a few deaths, to be mourned in the ship family; some damage, to be repaired expensively.

"Well," Picard said.

Riker nodded. "I would be tempted to say good riddance."

"Tempted," Picard said. "Yes. Anyway, those other ships are still out here . . ."

"Are you thinking that a wounded beast is the most dangerous?"

"Only in that it may have called friends," Picard said.

"They'll certainly take a while to get here."

"We hope they will," Picard said. "But right now, my main concern is for the ships in transit through this area—and I particularly want to have a look at *Boreal*, and make quite sure that they're all right."

"If they have had any little set-tos out here," Riker said, "perhaps earlier ones than the Lalairu had—"

"It could mean that the pirates are going to be more in evidence than usual. A good thing we're here."

"Depending," Riker said with a slight smile and

a glance out in Data's direction, "how you define *good.*"

"This is wonderful stuff," Captain Maisel was muttering at her end of the three-way link, as she looked over the beginnings of the Lalairu recordings and files. "Terrific . . ."

"What a data-hungry little creature you are," Clif said; but Picard watched him, too, scanning his output screen thoughtfully.

"Information is everything," Ileen said, "and out in these spaces, too often it costs blood. The free gift of it, when the Lalairu are likely enough to have shed enough of their own ichor or serum or whatever for it, is priceless."

"Well, it's going to take weeks to go through all this," Clif said. "But, Captains, if I may suggest it to you, probably we should now head after the bigger of those two pirate craft."

"I'd already reached that decision," said Picard. "Ileen?"

"With you two along, I'm sure I don't mind," Maisel said. "I don't know if this is the same raider vessel we've been hearing occasional rumors about, but if it is, I'll be delighted to meet it in present company. How long do you think it's going to take to catch up?"

From behind her, Pickup said, "At warp five, I'd estimate twenty-four hours, Captain. Twelve, if we're lucky."

"Let's make it so, then," Picard said.

Data nodded. "Laying in the course, Captain . . ."

Picard sat down. "Engage."

Swiftly the Lalairu ships fell away behind. "I'll be in my ready room for a while," said Picard when they were well under way. He turned in his seat. "Mr. Worf, I want to talk to those people on *Boreal*. You may have to keep at them to get them to answer . . . but I would sooner avoid the kind of greeting that the Lalairu ship received."

"I will keep at them, Captain," Worf said, "but as for the greeting . . . I would like to see them try."

Picard smiled slightly, got up, and headed for the ready room.

He was glad to have time to go over some of the Lalairu material himself. Data had already thoughtfully prepared an index with descriptions of some of the files in the material, and Picard scanned down it on his screen, having already told the computer to deselect any material of strictly astrophysical interest; Data was better equipped than he to deal with that sort of thing.

Archaeological information, though, that was another question. Picard had spent some time the previous evening going over abstracts of the information that *Marignano* had picked up on her tour of duty so far. Clif might say what he liked about a course looking like the drunken staggers, but Picard was beginning to think that this kind of approach had something to recommend it. Ileen had walked on the surfaces of planets Picard had only read about in archaeological journals. *The thought of being able to get out there—not just occasionally but almost* routinely—*and see such things, walk on such worlds, knee deep in the past* . . .

Picard saw with astonishment that Ileen and her crew on *Marignano* had discovered, or rediscovered, Enser—an ancient avian civilization. The avians apparently saw Kepler's Star from fairly near at hand when it went supernova and had construed the sudden mighty light in the sky as a sign of war in heaven. He was delighted to find that an old theory of his turned out to be true. Over the course of centuries, the avians had remade themselves—retooling their own biology from that of a planet-bound, oxygen-breathing species to one that ingested light and radiation in almost any form, using it to power the great winged bodies they built for themselves. And when they had all undergone the change, they launched themselves into the interstellar night to do battle with the universe for the soul of God.

Picard shook his head at the image, awed and amazed. Who knew how many of the Enser had made their way to Kepler's Star and died there like moths in a candle flame, destroyed by the excess of radiation, or glory, unnecessary martyrs to the forces of nature. But necessity, Picard thought, is in the eye of the beholder . . . even when the result was a species dead in the heart of a supernova, and an empty planet that would never hear their wing beats again.

And yet another world, a vast primeval forest—

The communicator chirped. "Captain," said Mr. Worf's voice, "I have a response from *Boreal.* As you said, I had to keep at them—they seem reluctant to communicate. The signal quality is not of the best, but they are not too far away."

"Put them on my screen, then."

"Sir, the communication is voice only."

"A problem at their end?"

"Not that I can detect."

Picard put up his eyebrows. "Very well. *Boreal,* this is Captain Jean-Luc Picard of the *Starship Enterprise.*"

There was a fizz and crackle of static, not unexpected, really, since this whole region of space was filled with ionization from Kepler's Star. "The pleasure is completely one-sided," said an annoyed voice at one end. "I told the other ship the other day, and I'll tell you now: we came out here to get away from you. We don't want you around us. Leave us alone."

"I would like to speak to the master of *Boreal,* please," Picard said, firmly but politely.

"He's not available," said the abrupt voice at the other end. "This isn't his shift. Just like you people to expect him here just because *you're* calling. You can speak to me."

"And who are you, please?"

"I'm the team leader of the Third Submission colony group," said the voice. "Our names aren't for outsiders to hear."

"How shall I address you, then?"

"I don't want you to address me. What do you think I am, a public meeting? I want you to stop bothering us."

"Sir," Picard said. "Team leader, if I may. You must understand that, as one of the Federation's starships on patrol in this area, I have a responsibility to—"

"You have *no* responsibility that we recognize," said the voice angrily. "Responsibility cannot be imposed from outside. It can only be assumed willingly, by those willing to make answer."

"Yes," Picard said, wondering what he was getting himself into. "And since *I* have to make answer to the Federation authorities—"

"We do not," said the team leader. "We had a run-in with some of your agents, or should I say spies, a few days ago, and we told them—"

"Yes, I've heard about what you told them," Picard said, just a little wearily, "and I must tell you for your own good that taking the same line with a starship might be a mistake. Now. The purpose of my call was to warn you of the presence of unfriendly forces in this area. The Lalairu craft that you attacked—"

"Those no-good transients! I might have known."

"The Lalairu are not the raiders," Picard said, much more wearily. "They attacked and wiped out a raider group not far from what we now judge to be your present position. Our concern right now is that the same raider group will come across you and—"

"If they try it, we'll take care of them," said the team leader. "We can take care of ourselves. You just ask your Lalairu."

"Actually, we did," Picard said, with a level of enjoyment that was probably inappropriate, "and you wouldn't be able to do anything about the raiders, if they *did* catch up with you. The Lalairu scanned your weaponry most conclusively, and you have something of a shortfall, considering what would be needed. This is therefore to inform you that we will be joining you within the next eight standard hours, just to satisfy ourselves of your continued safety. We will be glad to escort you to the planet to which you're heading—"

"No," said the team leader. "We don't need or want you anywhere near our new world. I suppose we can't stop you from rendezvousing with us . . . but we don't want you anywhere near our destination. Not that I expect you to understand why."

Picard was glad of that, because he didn't, and didn't think he was likely to. "Nevertheless," he said, more sharply, "we and our sister ships will be with you within eight standard hours. And I strongly suggest that you do *not* fire on us. Picard out."

Picard killed the link, took a moment to breathe in and out—surprised by the level of his own annoyance—then touched his communicator. "Mr. Data?"

"Sir—"

"Lock onto the source of that last communication. Lay in a course for them, and advise *Oraidhe* and *Marignano*. Tell them to keep scanning for the pirates—but we need to make this one stop first."

"I will do so, Captain."

Picard sighed and went back to looking at the list of planets and resources, of the strange, the unknown, the inexplicable, that Captain Maisel had put together. *There's enough here,* he thought, *to keep a man, a ship, any hundred people or twenty ships, busy for a hundred years. Maybe Ileen has the right of it. Maybe this is really the place to be—*

Chirp. "Jean-Luc!" It was the yoo-hoo voice that Maisel tended to use when she was excited. "We've got something hot on long-range scan. About light-cruiser size? Running at low warp? Engine signature doesn't look too good—"

"Mr. Data—course to the pirate vessel, as opposed to that for *Boreal?*"

There was a pause. "The raider is to the galactic northward as well, one eighty-five plus seven. Divergence is fifteen light-years in x axis, six in y."

"Lucky for *Boreal* they've got some distance between them," Picard said grimly.

"Course laid in, sir."

"Engage."

Picard went back to looking at his screen again. A few moments later, his door chimed.

"Come."

Mr. Worf came in, handed him a padd to examine: it had the shift's comm logs on it, along with various other routine information. Picard looked. Worf thanked him in his gruff baritone, and then asked if the captain would be needing anything else.

Picard thought briefly. "You might assist me by seeing what information you can find regarding this Third Submission colony: their philosophical background and so forth."

"And why their representative has the manners of a Romulan slorg," Mr. Worf said, frowning.

Picard leaned back in his seat. "I hesitate to prejudge him, Mr. Worf," said Picard. "Or, for that matter, the slorg. Inform *Boreal* of our revised time of rendezvous, and call me when we're on approach to the pirate vessel."

Chapter Three

THE BRIDGE SETTLED into the steady give-and-take of reports and updates that had become familiar over many chases. But one thing became clear to Picard quickly. They were catching up very fast.

"No change in their position?" he said to Riker after a while.

"None," Riker replied, looking over Data's shoulder at the console. "They're just sitting there."

"A rendezvous, perhaps?"

Data shook his head. "There is no evidence of other ships in the area, Captain. If it is a rendezvous, it is one they have missed. Or perhaps someone else has."

"Possibly waiting for a pickup from one of their support ships," said Riker.

Picard thought about that for a moment. "Shields," he said.

"Shields up."

Riker looked up at Worf. "Arm the phasers and photon torpedoes—"

"Armed," Worf said, in a tone of voice that suggested that they had been that way for some time now. "Ready to fire."

"Purely as a matter of caution," Picard said. *"Oraidhe?"*

"We're with you, Captain," said Clif's voice.

"Marignano?"

"I wouldn't put it past him to be playing possum, Jean-Luc," said Ileen's voice. "Not after the drubbing that the Lalairu gave him. If I were him, I'd play dead."

And indeed, that seemed to be what he was doing. "Still no movement—"

"None, Captain," said Data.

They all gazed at the screen, waiting. Picard felt once again the old familiar urge to get up and pace, and repressed it. He sat and waited for that first faint gleam of light—

"Visual coming now," Data said, "at extreme range."

They were diving into a star system. In the distance, the primary, a small type F, glinted a clear pale green. Just visible in its light, a spark, not moving relative to them or the star. Slowly, the spark grew brighter, the light it reflected from the primary spreading over and defining a shape.

"Dropping out of warp," Riker said. "Half impulse. Mr. Worf—"

"Ready, Commander."

Slowly *Enterprise* coasted in. The shape grew more and more clearly defined—one of those needly forms they had seen attacking the Lalairu ship. It was a narrow four-sided pyramid, drawn out long and thin. The ship was not quite motionless in space; it was tumbling slowly, more or less end-over-end.

"Do you want me to put a tractor on it, Captain?" said Worf.

Picard shook his head. "I'd sooner not take the chance that adding our own vectors to it might in some way damage our analysis. Let it tumble. Bring us alongside at about ten kilometers, and match."

"Aye, sir," Data said. Slowly the vessel's image in the viewscreen stabilized, while the starfield behind it began a slow and stately pinwheeling. From *Marignano*, Captain Maisel said, "Matching tumble, *Oraidhe.*"

"Confirmed," Captain Clif said. "Weapons locked on."

On the screen, *Marignano* and *Oraidhe* took up positions matching *Enterprise*'s on the far side of the pirate vessel, seeming to come to rest against the pinwheeling stars. "You'll want to check me on this," Maisel said from *Marignano*, "but I'm getting *very* low life-sign readings. Only one or two . . . but at the same time, my sensors would seem to indicate almost no biomass on this ship."

No bodies, then, Picard thought. *What can this mean?*

"Have we another *Marie Celeste* here?" said Captain Clif's voice, sounding somewhat bemused.

"I'm preparing away teams," said Maisel.

Picard nodded at Riker. "Number One, see to our own team's composition. Mr. Data, do our sensor readings confirm *Marignano*'s?"

"Present readings would indicate no more than five life signs on the vessel; possibly as few as one. I confirm also that biomass is strangely lacking."

Picard looked over the outside of the ship. Pirate vessels tended to be less aesthetic than purpose-built spacecraft; they were usually largely modular, with alterations made on them higgledy-piggledy at clandestine illegal refitment facilities out in the depths of space. As a result, their outsides frequently looked as if bits and pieces had been bolted on any which way. This one was somewhat in that school of design, and there were some odd irregularities: what seemed to be booster pods or demi-nacelles, attached around the base of the ship's spire. There were also curious scooped-out spots, pockmarks up and down the body of the vessel. Deck plates had been removed there at some point, and outer hull structures of the vessel altered to take objects meant to fit into those pockmarks. "Magnify," Picard said.

The screen obediently showed a closer view of

the pitted hull. Picard looked down into the most conveniently placed of the pockmarks and saw grapples, and something that looked like an access tube. "Life-pod arrays," he said to Riker.

"Yes, sir. And they're all empty," Riker said.

"So it would seem. . . . Is the away team ready?"

"The security contingent is just making its way to the transporter room, Captain. Dr. Crusher's on her way as well."

"Good; that one life sign is of great interest to me. Keep in touch, Number One. And I want images."

"Yes, sir," Riker said, heading for the turbolift.

When the transporter let him go, Riker found himself looking down a long, dimly lit hallway—low-ceilinged, narrow. Captain Maisel and her team—her science officer and six others, all heavily armed—stood halfway down that hall, watching as Riker drew his phaser and pushed ahead of the crewman carrying the imaging equipment.

"Anything interesting so far, Captain?" Riker asked.

Maisel and her science officer had their tricorders out and were scanning around them. The rest of the away team, armed, stood by. "That life sign is up a deck or so from us, I'd say."

Riker thought with mild unease of what his instructors had always said about attacking uphill; you were always at a disadvantage. *No choice, though . . .* "Let's see if we can find an access.

Thorsson," Riker said to one of his team, "get down to engineering, or what passes for it in here, and see what you can do about these lights. Also, see if there was any engine damage to cause this low-power state, or whether this is just a shut-down."

"Aye, sir—"

Dr. Crusher came up beside Riker, walking by him and looking thoughtfully at her tricorder. "Life readings?" Riker said, glancing over her shoulder at the device.

"Only that one," she said, making some adjustments to the tricorder.

That, more than anything else, had him wondering. *Hope these people haven't come up with some exciting new way to fool our sensors. This would be a great place to test it. No witnesses, way out here in the dark . . .* "How is it?"

Crusher shook her head. "Hard to tell until I see what's producing it. If the source of the reading is a humanoid, the reading's iffy. There's certainly an injury of some kind."

Riker nodded, glancing around him. "Keep sharp, people," he called to the group ahead of him. "We may have someone waiting in ambush."

The doorways were no more than a meter and a half high, and all were stuck shut; they had to be laboriously levered apart and slid open. Riker's heart started to pound as the door began to come open. He took a long breath, ready. The door opened. One of Maisel's armed people peered in first, then waved her captain forward. Maisel stepped into the doorway, glanced in. "Look at this, Mr. Riker—"

He did. The room was apparently someone's living quarters—a humanoid's, to judge by the furniture. Several drawers and a cupboard were open; items of clothing in some soft, shimmering material lay on the bed, as if casually tossed there.

"Not looted or rifled, I think," Maisel said. "Otherwise a lot more of these would be open."

Riker looked the place over. "Someone packing in a hurry—"

They went on. Riker headed after Crusher, who was making her way down the hall on the trail of the active life sign. The two parties came to the end of the hall and had to go on more slowly, since there were neither lifts nor stairs, only a narrow Jeffries tube to be climbed to the next level. Riker stood at the bottom of the tube as the first couple of security people put their heads up into the next level and looked warily around. "It's all right," one of them called. "Just like the one below."

The group began to make their way up. This hall was as dimly lit and cramped as the one beneath it, lined with the same short, shut doors.

"Thorsson to Riker—"

"Go ahead."

"Sir, we're in the ship's engine room. Kind of a cobbled-together place—" A pause. Riker swallowed. "Doesn't seem to be much damage, though. Nothing unusual down here, no sign of boobytraps. Otherwise, the ship's just been left running on reduced power, to save energy—not because of damage."

Riker let out another of those long breaths, relieved. "Can you get us some light in here?"

"We're working on it, sir. The controls are a little obscure—"

"All right, keep working on it." Riker went on after Maisel.

Dr. Crusher was pushing her way on up through those away team personnel who were ahead of her. "This way," she said. Several of the armed security people hurried to catch up with her.

Crusher eyed her tricorder, then took a few more paces down the dim hallway. Near one doorway, she put up a sudden hand. "Look," she said.

Riker looked at the spots on the floor: dark blue spots and a dark blue smudge on the doorframe. *Blood?* he wondered. "Blood," said Crusher, almost as if in response.

The doctor held up her tricorder and let it have a good look around, scanning the ceiling as well as the walls and floor. "All right," she said at last. "Don't touch any of those—there may be need for forensic work later. Someone come give me a hand with this—"

Abruptly the lights came up. Riker looked hurriedly around him, half expecting the ship's denizens, hiding until now, to come boiling out of the closed doors like some deadly surprise party. But there was no other change, no sound except that of their own breath and footsteps.

"All right," Riker said then, waving his people forward. He and Maisel came up close behind Crusher as one of *Marignano*'s security people got busy levering and pushing the door open. It stuck and screeched dreadfully.

The room was storage of some kind, its walls lined with cabinets and closets. Against the lower tier of cabinets on the left side of the room, someone—a humanoid figure—lay crumpled. More dark blue was spattered around and smeared on the cupboard door.

Riker watched Crusher go over to kneel by the faintly breathing shape, still keeping an eye on her tricorder. "It's an Alpheccan," she said.

"He's a long way from home," Riker said, somewhat surprised.

Dr. Crusher gave him a sidewise glance and said, "And *we're* not?" She reached over the Alpheccan's shoulders to pull him carefully back into a leaning position against her. He wore a dark coverall, the upper right side of which was smeared and sodden with blue from a gaping chest wound. The normal navy blue of his skin was paled almost to cerulean. His eyes were open, even the nictitating membranes contracted out of the way, so that the violet orbs of the inner eye looked sightlessly out into the hallway, past Riker and the crewman with the imaging device. But there was no sign of consciousness in those eyes. Riker shivered.

Picard leaned back in his seat, looking up at the screen, now divided between the away team's view and a view of *Oraidhe*'s bridge. "The question, now," he said to Clif, with whom he had been talking while watching the teams finish their work, "is what to do with this vessel."

"Well," Clif said, looking slightly quizzical, "its crew has abandoned it. By the laws of salvage, it belongs to anyone who now comes along to claim it. *We* could do so . . . but frankly, Captain, I don't relish the idea of dragging this thing along after us while we're on patrol."

"Jean-Luc," said Ileen from the bridge of *Marignano,* "if you feel you might want to have another look at it later, why not just leave a sensor buoy with it, set to notice if anyone comes along and shows interest. If anyone does, the buoy can notify us . . . and also broadcast a message that this vessel is under investigation." She sat down in her center seat and smiled a big, bright, sunny smile. "You might even slap a Q on it."

"Quarantine?" Clif said, acquiring a rather artificial look of shock.

Picard smiled a little bit himself. "Weren't you telling us, Ileen, that some of the settled worlds in this area had been troubled by sporular angue fever?"

Captain Maisel nodded innocently. "Virulent stuff, that. And opportunistic. Four systems down with it, at least."

The three captains nodded gravely at one another. Riker, who had come in partway through the discussion, smiled a very sideways smile, touched his commbadge, and started having a quiet discussion with someone in engineering about a marker buoy.

"Protective measures aside," Maisel said, "if I came across a ship like this, in this part of space, when all kinds of people have heard the kinds of stories about this area that I have, I wouldn't want anything to do with the thing. I'd leave it right where it was."

"We might as well do the same, for the moment," Clif said. "We have other concerns."

"Agreed," Picard said. "More than ever, now, I'm eager to touch base with the people on that colony ship; I want to make sure they get where they're going safely."

"Yes," Clif and Maisel said almost in unison.

"Let's make it so, then. Mr. Data—"

"Laying in a course, Captain, and datastreaming it to *Marignano* and *Oraidhe.*"

"Very good. Let's go. If anyone wants me, I'll be down in sickbay."

The Alpheccan lay on one of the diagnostic beds, the screen above it showing a most unusual internal arrangement of which Picard could make out absolutely nothing. Crusher was standing with her arms folded, a whole range of diagnostic tools lying to one side on a table while she gazed thoughtfully at the screen. Standing next to her was a tall balding man with an open, friendly face.

"Captain," said Crusher. "Oh, Captain, this is Dr. Spencer, Jim Spencer, from *Marignano.*"

Picard nodded to him. "Pleased," he said,

"He's worked with Alpheccans before; I haven't really," Crusher said.

"Clinic work mostly, on Alphecca Four," said Spencer. "But they're not that common a people outside their own system. Normally they don't care for star travel much—religious and cultural reasons. However, as you see, there are always exceptions to the rule."

Picard nodded, looking at the screen again. "Correct me if I'm wrong, but he—he?—appears to have two of everything."

"Nearly," Spencer said. "With the possible exception of the brain, which would seem to be bad luck for this gentleman."

"Why? What's the matter?"

"Well—" Crusher gestured them all away from the bed, and they walked into her office, waited for the doors to shut. "He's dying, Captain; I'm afraid there's no question about that. I could prolong the process, but ethically I'd be on shaky ground."

"The problem," said Spencer, "is not so much that he's dying, but that, as he is at the moment, he shouldn't be alive at all."

"He seems to have incurred some kind of brain damage," said Crusher. "And it's a very peculiar kind, because in terms of actual trauma to his analogue of the cerebrum and cerebellum, there *is* none. His autonomic nervous system is perfectly intact . . . except that it seems not to be working properly. It's slowly losing function, giving up the business of running his breathing and heartbeat, and the process would seem to be irreversible. When I have to sign his death certificate—something I'm pretty sure I'm going to have to handle in the next few hours—the proximate cause of death will be heart failure secondary to cerebellar dysfunction. But that will *not* be what killed him. I don't know what did."

Picard sat down, concerned. "Some kind of weapon, perhaps?" he said. "Or exposure to radiation?"

Crusher and Spencer shook their heads in unison. "No chance, Captain," said Spencer, "or very little. The only weapon this man had any contact with would have been someone's blaster or disruptor. That damage we repaired. But no known radiation, or infectious agent, can cause these effects."

"The problem is that this Alpheccan's brain is *intact*, Captain," Crusher said, sitting down on her desk and staring at her screen as if simply staring could make it give up some answers. "It has no reason to be failing. Its electrical action is somewhat reduced, but that clinical sign could be commensurate with the effects of shock. While the patient suffered considerable blood loss, that's been replaced, and the loss alone wasn't enough to cause the profound unconsciousness we see here, or, for that matter, to cause any kind of significant brain damage—that kind of trauma leaves detectable signs in the cerebral vascularization."

There was a soft *chirp* from the screen. Crusher looked out of her office toward one of her staff who was standing by the bed with an instrument in his hands and a "yes or no?" expression on his face. "Half a second," she said, and went out.

When she came back, her face told the story. "That's it," Crusher said. "His dorsal heart just stopped for the third time, and his ventral one hasn't been working for the last hour. I told Mike not to bother with another restart; it serves no purpose."

Picard nodded sadly.

Crusher sighed and sat down in her chair. "Captain, if you're looking for a fast diagnosis from me, I don't have one for you. We'll get started on the autopsy right away. Jim, have you got time to spare?"

"Plenty. I'll gown up."

"Analysis is going to take a while, Jean-Luc," Crusher said. "When I run into a clinical picture this barren, I don't like to rush. If you'll check with me tomorrow about this time, I may have some initial indications for you. But I have to say, I can't guarantee much of anything."

"All right, Doctor," Picard said, getting up. "Let me know if anything of interest comes up before then."

He went out past the Alpheccan, glancing only briefly at him as he passed. It might have been a trick of the somewhat subdued lighting in sickbay, or the dark complexion, or something about the way the Alpheccan's face was shaped, but Picard could not get rid of the impression that that face wore the faintest shadow of a smile. Coupled with the dark, empty eyes, it was an uncanny effect. He went out, turning the situation over in his mind. *One more mystery . . . one more among too many, for so early in the mission.*

. . . I don't like it. Snug in your quarters with a book, or down in the holodeck, mysteries could be pleasant enough. But this far out in space, out here in the empty places, they could turn lethal with great speed.

He headed for the bridge, where mysteries at least unfolded themselves in better lighting.

An hour or so later, Picard sat in his ready room, finishing a very belated lunch and reading the material that Mr. Worf had managed to compile for him on the Third Submission colony.

It made interesting and rather distressing reading. The group seemed to be on a planet of 60 Ophiuchi, a planet called Errigal. Errigal itself had been settled by humanoid stock, though from very different origins: Andorians and humans.

The migrants' dominant faith was called Dahna by its adherents. It was a faith with a profound certainty of its own rightness—something Picard had noticed all too many religions possessing. Worse, from Picard's point of view, this particular faith taught that the natural universe was a pure and unpolluted place, but that the doings of sentient creatures polluted it.

Picard sat back in his chair and sighed, listening briefly to the faint bubbling of the aerator in the fishtank, and wondering at the bizarre logic of this worldview. The Dahna Andorians were sure that the universe should have remained lifeless, that the stars should have burned in pristine glory, their planets untroubled by the arrogant, destructive, semifungal growth known as life. Such a universe, untroubled though it might be, struck Picard as a deadly dull sort of place . . . not that the one *he* inhabited was perfect, by any stretch of the imagination. Nonetheless, the Dahna adherents saw the incursion and pullulation of life through the universe as a horrible error. Some of their religious writings eagerly described the possibility of time travel, in terms of evolving a missionary society whose business would be to trace back, to the dawn of time and life, the germination of that first cell in some primordial ocean, with an eye to wiping it out and retroactively destroying all life, including themselves. You had to give them that, Picard thought: they were even-handed, if nothing else.

Lacking time machines, the Dahna adherents'

goal became to take themselves far away from other cultures and life, to live in the plainest way possible, enjoying life as little as they could, creating nothing—for creation was blasphemy, part of the dreadful tumorous tendency of life to reproduce itself—and in all ways trying to achieve a lifestyle that mostly involved sitting still, subsisting, and waiting to die.

Picard's second cup of tea got cold, and the fishtank bubbled on, the lionfish inside it bumping incuriously against the glass and gracefully waving its tan-and-cream-striped spines. It was no wonder, Picard thought, that such people would see him as practically a demonic figure, and the *Enterprise* and her sister starships as symbolic of everything they stood against—of doing and being in the universe, of asserting one's own right to exist and to work out what life should be, what was worth desire and passion and energy. *All those things were evils to them. I must take the greatest care to be nonjudgmental about this,* he thought. But he had a feeling this time he was going to find it harder than usual.

"Captain?" Data's voice sounded tinny through the filter of the commbadge.

"Yes, Mr. Data."

"We are within sensor range of *Boreal.*"

"Very well. Advise them that a small party will be over to visit within the hour."

"Sir," said Data, "they seem disinclined to host guests."

"I understand that," said Picard. "But let them know that they will have them."

When the transporter's light died away and the singing whine went silent, Picard, Worf, and Troi found themselves in a surprisingly big, airy space.

Picard looked up at a big curving metal sky, set at intervals with lighting panels that shed a cool light over everything. The total effect was of an omnidirectional glow: shadows struck in all directions, and they were faint, washed out by closer sources of illumination. Here and there a clump of blocks made a "housing development" or tiny hamlet. Elsewhere were small patches of green—gardens, lawns, groves of hydroponically sustained trees—and patches of color that indicated plants from worlds where the chlorophyll had preferred other colors than green.

Near where the landing party stood was a clump of trees that could have been mistaken for a small park. There was even a park bench, and sitting on it a man watching them. Troi glanced at him, then turned around casually to look at another grove of trees surrounding what were probably several living blocks. "Here's our host, Captain," she said softly, "if that's the word I'm looking for."

The man on the bench got up, came to them. He was tall, fit-looking, extremely handsome, and to judge by the lines in his face, in his mature years, though exact age was hard to tell. He was a palecomplected, dark-haired man, dressed in a simple beige coverall and a frown.

He stopped a short distance away from them, as if they might have some sort of contagious disease. "You're Captain Picard," he said.

"And you, if I'm not mistaken, would be the team leader."

"Yes. Captain, I can't really say that we appreciate your effort in following us here. For my own people's sake, I'd thank you to keep your own visit here as brief as possible. I have their spiritual welfare to consider as well as their physical wellbeing, and stopping for this meeting with you has required energy expenditures we weren't planning."

"I will keep things as brief as our concerns make possible," Picard said, and they began to walk along a path that wound through several small groups of living cubes.

As they walked, Troi looked over into another little patch of parkland. There were some children there, but they were not running or playing; they sat, very still and quiet, looking down at the grass. The whole place had that same kind of breathless quiet about it, unbroken by any sound but that of the blowers that kept the air fresh and substituted for wind. The people that the *Enterprise* away team passed were walking slowly, steadily, without any great animation. It was hard to believe, in that silence, that anyone could laugh.

"Frankly, team leader," Picard said, "I'm glad to find you, your people, and your ship in one piece. There are some very odd things going on out in these spaces."

"The sooner you let us go on about our business, then," said the team leader, "the sooner we'll be safe on our chosen planet, where such things will be much less likely to happen."

"I very much doubt that," said Picard, wondering as they walked whether the man actually believed what he was saying. "I have reason to believe that your ship is in danger of falling afoul of the same force or forces who dealt with the pirate craft that we've just come across." As briefly as possible, Picard told the team leader about the condition in which they had found that vessel. "I have a certain interest," Picard said finally, "in making sure the same fate does not befall your people."

"That being the case—"

"I have an awful feeling I know what you're about to say," said Picard, being careful to keep his growing annoyance out of his voice. "You need to understand, however, that I need to know the details about where you're going."

"Captain," said the team leader with exaggerated patience, "that's information I will not give you, as I said before. You're intruding grievously on our rights of passage—"

"Those rights obtain within Federation space,"

Picard said mildly. "But in *these* spaces, there is no law to guarantee or enforce such rights—especially in emergency situations."

"Captain," said the team leader, throwing a look at Worf that was less than friendly, "I will not—"

"Let me be quite clear with you," said Picard. "I have no desire to follow you to your planet of choice. I understand your desire to have us stay away from it. I am willing to honor that . . . but only if you will be reasonable and divulge your true destination. Should anything happen to you— loved ones left behind, family, friends—will at least have a way to discover what happened to you."

"All the family and friends that we want are here with us," the team leader said.

On a walkway a few hundred yards distant, past a clump of containerized trees, a group of children hurried by—the first quick motion Picard had seen since they had been there, and one that drew his attention almost against his will. Behind the children came a young woman, in another of the plain coveralls, desperately hissing at the children to slow down and walk properly. The children were ignoring her; one actually laughed, the sound echoing so that it sounded much bigger than it really was, and Picard felt briefly like applauding.

He restrained himself, turning his attention back to the team leader. But the man simply looked away from him, as if waiting for him to leave.

Picard sighed. "If you refuse to inform us of your destination, I'm afraid I must tell you I will slap a tractor on your vessel and sit here with you indefinitely. You will go no farther, and you can complain to Starfleet until you've turned the color of your choice. But I warn you that I doubt they'll take any intransigence on your part very kindly."

The team leader stopped in his tracks and stared at Picard with an expression that was actually admiring, in a cockeyed kind of way. "You really think you're right, don't you?" he said, almost sadly. "That you're doing good. You honestly believe that." He sighed and looked away. "I would try to reason with you and show you the error of your ways—but time's wasting, and I don't know if I have that many years."

Picard held his peace and kept his face quite still through this. He felt he was being upgraded from the "dimwitted child" category to that of a benighted savage, but one with qualities that might be worth saving.

"Captain, perhaps I can save you some time," the team leader finally said. "Our destination is Fourteen-forty Ophiuchi B Five."

Picard stole a quick sideways glance at Troi. She didn't return the look, which he took as confirmation that the man was probably telling the truth. "I thank you for that, team leader," he said, and they walked on.

"It's a very nice planet, really," said the team leader. "Fertile—a big temperate band. Not much in the way of oceans, but we don't mind that. Mammals are in short supply there—we've brought a few, and some insects to pollinate the plants. As for the rest—" He shrugged. "You take your chances, settling a new world."

"Yes. I hope you do well there."

"I take your thought kindly, Captain," said the team leader, "though our concept of doing well and yours are probably fairly different."

When the details were resolved, the team leader simply turned and walked away. (There were no good-byes.) Silent, the away team beamed back up; as they went, Picard looked one last time off in the direction toward which the children had run, and listened, in vain, for any last echo.

As the transporter room reformed around them, Picard looked at Troi.

"Are you all right, Counselor?"

She laughed, a short, harsh sound. "Captain, I may complain sometimes about the turmoil of the emotions of people around me. And I'm well enough protected that I can normally cope with what's going on. But I'd sooner deal with a whole shipful of angry or crazy people than that psychic dead space over there. The bondage . . . it's not even pain: they've been suppressing it so long that there's very little left but a dull ache." She shook her head. "The planet he identified—"

"He was telling the truth, then?"

"As far as I can tell. I got a clear sense that his respect for you increased somewhat when you let him know that you'd caught him in a lie."

"That's one thing research is good for, anyway," said Picard. "Well, we'll pass this new information on to Mr. Data. Mr. Worf, set the communications schedule up, and they can go on their way."

"Yes, sir."

Troi and Worf went out of the transporter room ahead of Picard. He thought a moment, and then headed for sickbay.

It was nearly empty when he got there; they were having a quiet time. Crusher was back in her office, tapping away at her monitor, pausing every now and then to speak to the screen.

Picard strolled through, nodded to a crewman having his arm patched up by one of Crusher's assistant doctors, and tapped on the doorframe of Crusher's office. The doctor looked up, crooked a finger at him; he came in.

"Sit down, Jean-Luc. I'm almost done with this."

"And this is what?"

"Oh, the autopsy information on—" She nodded out at the diagnostic bed where the Alpheccan had lain.

"Any indication of the cause of the brain damage?"

She pushed the padd aside and leaned on her elbows on the desk. "No, and truly it's a puzzle. Not that it was damage as such, Jean-Luc. I looked for it right down to the molecular level: nothing." She gazed at the wall across from her, as if expecting to find answers there. "I looked most carefully at the possibility of some causative organism or infectious agent, some kind of DNA derangement or . . ." She shrugged. "I may be missing something. But I don't think so. I think this is simply something we've never seen before, and I *hate* coming up with something we've never seen before. Not when it's something like this."

She shuddered, and Picard thought of Troi. "Well," he said, "of course you'll let me know if you come up with anything."

"A sudden attack of genius wouldn't hurt," Crusher said, somewhat morosely. "I'm going to sit down and have a long talk with Jim Spencer to make sure this isn't something that's turned up in the Alpheccan literature previously. But he seemed as confused as I am." She gave Picard a rueful smile. "Which makes me feel slightly better, though not that much."

Picard nodded. "It's interesting," he said, "to have people outside our own ship to consult with, for a change. Exploring the far reaches by yourself can have its points, but so does traveling in company every now and then. Which reminds me—"

His commbadge chirped; he tapped it. "Picard here."

"Captain," said Data, "as you requested, I have checked our records of the remote probe sensor readings on Fourteen-forty Ophiuchi B Five. They confirm the presence of an M-zero type planet in the Bodean optimum-orbit range for the star in question, a G-eight, and on initial examination the planet would seem favorable for colonization—interglaciated and temperate. There are some slight oddities in the planet's temperature data, but the remote probe that was responsible for the survey was also manifesting some difficulties with its IR sensor cluster at the time, possibly accounting for the anomalies."

"Are these anomalies serious enough to be a cause for concern?" said Picard.

"From the present data, I would think not."

"I commend your thoroughness, Mr. Data. Meanwhile, unless the other captains have some other business that needs attending to, we should now set our course to follow the remaining pirate vessel."

"That course is laid in and awaits your order, Captain. As regards other business, Captain Clif advised us a short time ago that he would be beaming over to see you within the hour."

"Yes," Picard said. "Engage, then; and when the captain comes aboard, ask him to meet me in Holodeck Twelve."

"Yes, Captain."

Dr. Crusher looked at Picard with a slight smile

as he stood up from the desk. "Business?" she said. "A strategy meeting?"

"Hardly." Picard gave her a wry look. "You're the one who's always telling me that I need more recreational time. Well, haven't I been seeing to that lately?"

She raised her eyebrows at him. "You've been making more of an effort, I admit," she said. "I'll let you know when I think it's reached therapeutic levels, Jean-Luc, but so far I haven't seen any indication that you're overdoing it."

"I'll expect you to let me know if I do. Meanwhile, though—as I was saying, we don't often get much chance to socialize with other ships' crews. Clif's an interesting person—"

"Or persons."

"Yes," Picard said. "I suppose you could put it that way." He didn't speak the rest of his thought—that there hadn't been much chance for him, at least, ever to get to know a Trill well. Beverly had done so, and Picard wasn't sure that he cared, right this minute, to investigate how she felt these days about that old encounter.

Beverly, though, just smiled slightly and said, "Go on, Jean-Luc, and confer and otherwise confabulate with your fellow captain. If I come across anything here that you need to know about in a hurry, I'll let you know."

Picard nodded and went out.

* * *

It was coming on toward sunset; the water had gone three-colored, the waves golden on their swell side and red-golden on their lees, and in the restless space between waves a cerulean blue mirrored the highest sky, untouched by the sunset.

Picard and Clif walked along the deck of the frigate, Clif a little more slowly than Picard as he got used to the slight roll of the ship. The oncoming evening was quiet; the occasional seabird's cry was distant, drifting from the direction of the low, humpbacked island that hunched against the eastern horizon. Around them, ropes creaked and canvas flapped slack in the warm wind as sail was taken off. Various crewmen in the shipboard wear of nineteenth-century Earth touched their caps to the two captains as they went up and down the deck about their business. Up near the bow, several crewmen were down on their knees, enthusiastically holystoning the deck; amidships, a group of ten or so were going through gun drill.

Picard and Clif paused to watch them, leaning on the rail that looked toward the sunset-gilded island, a kilometer or two away.

"Thirty-pounders," Picard said. "Not the heaviest that a ship like this might carry, but adequate for the work: and you don't want to handicap your vessel's nimbleness in a fight by overgunning yourself."

The crew carefully adjusted the guns so that they were parallel to the ship's deck, and held them there, an interesting business while the ship rolled. "Take out your tompions—"

"I think I prefer the way we do it now," Clif said with a smile, as the gun crew pulled stoppers out of the guns' muzzles. "Less shouting, anyway."

Picard chuckled. "Oh, I don't know; even the shouting has its uses. The release of tension—"

"Load cartridge!"

Cartridges of black powder were rammed down the open muzzles. "And we're keeping a lost art alive," Picard said. "If *art* is the word we're looking for here."

"Shot your guns—" Clif braced himself against the rail, but nothing happened except that gun-crew members came up with thirty-pound cannon-balls and loaded them into the guns' muzzles. "Run out your guns!"

The crews put their shoulders to the cannons' carriages and pushed them out with a rush, so that all the muzzles protruded from the ship's side at the same time. "Prime!" Other members of the crews leaned forward over their fellows, bracing the guns, to pour more black powder into the cannons' touch holes. "Point your guns!"

"Now, then," Picard said softly. At the rear of each gun, a crewman held a hissing, smoking slow match to the breech of the gun while the cannons' angles were given one last adjustment. "Elevate— fire!"

The whole ship shook as the guns fired on the

uproll; thick white smoke, briefly shot through with sparks, was everywhere. Coughing came out of the smoke, and someone said loudly, "Well, what was the time?"

A pause. "Thirty-three seconds."

The gun crew cheered raggedly as the smoke started to clear. Picard stepped away from the rail, as much to get out of the smoke as anything else, and Clif came with him as he paused by the leader of the gun crew.

"I beg to report to the captain," said the young dark-haired man, "that we've improved our time by fifteen percent."

Picard nodded. "Nicely done, Mr. Moore," he said. "I'm sure *Trafalgar* will be much improved by your work. Carry on."

The two captains made their way back to the stern, where there were benches convenient to the wheel. No one manned it, in this near-flat calm; it was lashed to its capstan. Picard had a look at the lashings before he sat down.

"This great love that humans have for the old," Clif said, leaning back against the rail. "I've seen it before; some of my own human crew seem to share it. I have to confess it's a bit of a mystery to me."

Picard sat listening to the chuckle of the water under the keel for a few seconds. "Probably it's a mystery to some humans as well," he said. "The past has its own cachet because of its inaccessibility."

"And so we desire what we cannot have," Clif

said. "Except, of course"—and he glanced around him—"we *can* have it now."

The look he gave Picard then was almost sly, like a teacher watching to see if a student will fall into a trap. Picard laughed out loud. "Oh, come on, now, Captain," he said. "I don't think our species' definitions of reality are quite that different. And you would hardly be a captain in Starfleet if your personal definition was."

Clif nodded, smiled slightly. "Point taken. And call me Clif, if you like."

"I'm Jean-Luc, then."

"Very well, and I thank you." He brushed a fallen spark from one of his sleeves and said, bemused, "Your people really wore things like this in battle?"

"Some were a lot more ornate," Picard said. "You should see the French ones; these are fairly sedate by comparison."

"Fascinating."

They both glanced up then as, slow and low, a broad-winged shadow planed overhead between them and the quarter-moon: an albatross. It glanced at them with one cool dark eye as it went over, clattered its big beak a couple of times, and took itself leisurely off northward.

A sharp metallic sound echoed down the length of the deck. Picard looked in that direction, then frowned. "Mister," he called. "What is it? Brand? You uncock that crossbow this minute. Mr. Moore, put him on report."

"Aye, sir."

Clif looked with some amusement at Picard's wry expression. "He wouldn't really have shot it, would he?"

"In here," Picard said, "it's sometimes difficult to tell. A lot of the people who enjoy this scenario are very sensitive to archetype."

Another crewman, a slender, handsome, sharp-faced woman with long black hair tightly braided, came up to the stern deck carrying a pair of leather bottles, which she handed to the captains with a nod, and went off again. Clif looked at his with interest. "Refreshments? Thank you, Jean-Luc."

"À votre santé," Picard said. He uncorked his bottle and swigged. Clif followed suit and then spluttered abruptly.

"Goodness," he managed to say after a moment. "Sweeter than I expected. And stronger."

"Officers' rum doesn't get watered," Picard said with mild satisfaction. "Grog is for middies."

" 'Grog,' " Clif said reflectively. "Terrifying stuff. Do you serve snacks as well?"

"Salt beef. Hardtack. Or rather, ship's biscuit. With weevils or without?"

Clif blinked. "Which is preferable?"

Picard leaned back. "You'll hear aficionados arguing both sides of the case. Some favor the weevils for reasons of historical accuracy, others because they feel that a biscuit so bad it *doesn't* have weevils can't possibly have any nourishment left in it."

"One question. What's a weevil?"

Picard told him. Clif laughed uproariously; then the two of them sat quiet for a few minutes, watching the twilight.

Clif hiccupped, and hiccupped again. "Oh, dear," he said. *"Hic."*

Picard smiled and leaned back. "Hold your breath," he said. "Or have some more rum. It's just respiratory acidosis, so our ship's surgeon tells me. A good dose of sugar, or more carbon dioxide, will increase the acidosis enough to put you right."

Clif opted for the rum. After another drink, his eyes were watering slightly. "Sweet powers—*hup*—what do they make this stuff out of?"

"Sugar cane, I believe. A local plant. Fermented and then distilled a couple of times, or more. Helps it go down more smoothly."

" 'Goes down,' *hup,* is a euphemism. I'm going to need to have my throat checked."

"Oh, you'll be all right, I think. See, they've stopped."

"So they have. What a relief."

"Surely hiccups aren't very serious."

"Not for *you,* maybe. But the symbiont pouch is right under the diaphragm. How would *you* like it if the bag you were stuffed into suddenly started being squeezed from all sides and shaken repeatedly?"

The air whistled. "Captain Picard?"

"Yes, Mr. Data."

"Sir, I have managed to make contact with the

second survey probe, and have pulled its data on the system to which the *Boreal* colonists are making their way."

Picard blinked. If he didn't know better, he would think he heard a note of urgency in the android's normally placid voice.

The captains stood up together, bracing themselves against the swell, which was picking up as the evening inshore breeze began to rise. "Perhaps," Clif said, "you'd make me a copy of this program. It looks like a nice place to visit."

"It is," Picard said, watching as the gun crew began preparing for another timed run. "Computer, end program, save, copy to the computers on *Oraidhe,* to the attention of Captain Clif."

The holodeck computer chirped acquiescence. And it all went away—the violet sea, the wind, the albatross's cry, the evening star in the royal blue sky, and young crossbow-toting Brand looking up at it thoughtfully as he leaned back against the mainmast. All gone in a breath, nothing left but dark walls and bright gridlines, and the scent of bougainvillea on some tropical breeze. Clif, who had been looking back at Brand, blinked as he vanished.

They went out into the corridor together. Clif said, "They don't seem able to do anything about aromas, do they?"

Picard shook his head. "My chief engineer told me it has something to do with 'short particularity' in humanoid olfactory systems. He tried explaining, but I decided about that point there were some things that captains didn't need to know." He grinned. "The blowers will clear it out shortly. The extra system's a blessing, especially after Mr. Worf staged one of his Klingon banquets."

The turbolift doors closed.

Chapter Four

CLIF AND PICARD stood behind Data's console and
watched him call up the information from the
sensor probe on the front viewscreen.

On the main viewscreen, an image sprang into
being: first the primary of the star system and a
dim spark well out from it, then a series of rapidly
closing-in "frames" of the spark, during which it
enlarged from dust mote to tiny spangle to silver-
blue cloud-swirled coin. Finally, it appeared up
close as a handsome-looking planet, wearing a big
equatorial sea skewed across its equator, with a
brace of ruddy moons in tow. "This," Data said,
"is the original information."

"Nice-looking place," said Clif.

Picard nodded. "Typical M-type. A dead-on
zero, I'd say."

"And here," Data said, "is the visual data from a second probe I sent for confirmation."

There was the primary again, with its characteristic golden-green gleam; it was a hard star to miss, once you were used to the slightly unusual hue. But the secondary spark was missing. The screen leaped in close, and closer, as the earlier view had, but there was no sign of a planet where there should have been one.

Picard looked at the screen and shook his head. "A malfunction?" he said. "Some orbital anomaly, perhaps?"

"No, Captain."

The two captains stood looking at the empty space and glanced at each other. "I have had difficulty establishing which information is correct. Both probes' own diagnostics check out to the last checksum digit. Each probe is certain it 'saw' the result you have seen," Data said.

"No chance of any kind of planetary collision, I suppose," Clif said. "The system would still be cluttered with the debris."

"Correct, sir."

"You're quite sure the star is the same?" Picard said.

"The spectrography matches exactly, Captain," Data said. "There is no chance of error."

Picard folded his arms and gave Clif a thoughtful look. "Well," he said, "this raises a new set of problems. There's no way to tell which of these data sets is accurate. Certainly one would prefer it was the one that shows a planet. But if that planet is not there—" He shook his head. "Colonization ships rarely carry much more food and other raw materials than they need for the actual journey to their destination. If the *Boreal*'s colonists arrive at this star and find there's no planet there, they're going to need help. At least when it comes to provisions, even if they won't let us take their personnel on board."

"I concur, Captain. I'm sure Ileen will as well."

"Mr. Data," Picard said, "how long will it take us, at optimum warp, to catch up with *Boreal?*"

He glanced at his panel for a moment. "Eight hours, forty minutes, Captain."

"Lay in the course, then, and make it so."

Not quite eight hours later, Picard was back on the bridge. Data looked up from his panel as the captain came in.

"Report," Picard said.

"On one matter at least," said Data, "we now have certainty. The Vulcans will need to look into the way their scan data are protected. We will reach the primary within forty minutes. However, long-range scan indicates no planet in orbit around it."

Riker came onto the bridge at that point, looked around, saw Picard, and came down to him with an alert look in his eye. "No planets," he said.

"So I hear, Number One."

"Someone," said Riker, "went to some trouble over all this. Not just faking one planet, but faking the presence of all the others. They even put the target planet in the correct Bodean relationship to the others."

Picard nodded. "Not all species use Bode's Law," he said, "or recognize it as a law as such. But many humanoid species do use it to a greater or lesser extent, probably a majority. Mr. Data?"

"I would concur, Captain. Approximately seventy percent of humanoid species find that particular set of ratios useful or attractive in terms of their native forms of mathematics."

"So," said Ileen Maisel's voice suddenly—apparently she had been eavesdropping. "This subterfuge, if it is one, might be directed at humanoids specifically?"

"That is more than we could say from the present information, Captain . . . but a possibility nonetheless."

"Ileen, do your sensors show you anything more than ours do?" Picard asked.

"A lot of empty space right now, Jean-Luc. Also, my science officer suggests to me that there's something funny going on with the *Boreal*'s ion trail."

"Mr. Data, have you been looking at it?"

"So far I have not noticed anything out of the ordinary. Attenuation seems appropriate for the projected speed and time. However—" He examined his panel, worked at it for a moment. The schematic of the ion trail's route through space appeared on the main viewscreen, corkscrewing off into the distance. Near the end of it, faint, enhanced by the computer graphic, was an abrupt faint segment of straight line, intersecting with the visible end of the *Boreal*'s trail and fading away.

"About fifteen minutes to the primary," Data said.

"Acknowledged," came Clif's voice from *Marignano*. And then, after a moment, *"Enterprise, would you check some data for us, please?"*

"Certainly, Captain."

Marignano's science officer said, "There was certainly another ship through here, sirs, though I think *ship* may be the wrong word. *Vessel,* perhaps. I almost wouldn't know *what* to call it, to judge by the warp flux residues it's left."

Picard, his eyebrows up, had to agree. *"Boreal*'s trail," he said to Data. "Could that be what we're seeing?"

Data's hands danced over his console for a moment, but then he shook his head. "After its enclosure by the larger field," he said, "it fades out rapidly."

"But no sign of its destruction—"

"No, Captain. None."

"Nasty," Ileen's voice said. "Swoop down, pick up the ship whole, take it somewhere else to pick its bones . . ."

"Captains," Picard said, "may we have a brief conference in private?"

"No problem," Ileen said, and Clif said, "Right away."

Picard got up, gestured toward his ready room. "I'll take it in there, Mr. Worf."

The door closed behind him. He sat down at his desk, and the desk screen obligingly split its image to show him Maisel on one side, Clif on the other.

"Captain," said Clif, "you'll be thinking the same thing I am, I suspect. Do we have enough firepower, even among the three of us, tactically, to take on a vessel engined this way?"

"Just because it's got big engines," Ileen said, "doesn't necessarily mean it's got big weapons."

Picard put his eyebrows up in amusement at the sound of Ileen's eternal eagerness. "All the same," Clif said, "this far out in the middle of nowhere, I feel less than usually inclined to give the universe, or an unknown species, the benefit of the doubt. Even though we have no positive proof that this vessel's intentions are belligerent—for all we know, the *Boreal* may have been in some kind of distress—I'd still bet on it."

Ileen sighed. "I'd have to agree with you there. And as for whether or not we have the firepower to take on this other vessel, should it prove to be belligerent, I don't think we have a choice. They're our people. We have to go after them."

That, Picard thought, was Ileen all over. He just hoped they would be able to back her certainty with force. "Agreed," he said. "Not that that was ever really in question, I think. But no matter how superior an advantage this vessel might have in weapons, we still have a strategic or tactical advantage. We are three. It is only one—as far as we can tell."

Clif nodded, then turned his head. "Captain," his helm officer said from behind him, "long-range scan is showing something."

"The big ship?"

"No, sir. It might be *Boreal*. The size looks right—it's about three kiloparsecs out."

Ileen looked faintly outraged and glanced over her shoulder at her exec. "Now, why didn't we see that first—" she started saying, just as her exec said, "Captain, we've got it, too—"

"Never mind," Ileen said. "Let's go, gents."

The other two captains broke the link. Picard went out onto the bridge.

The viewscreen was already showing the tiny chip of light, more an example of wishful thinking in the computer's "mind" than of any real image, so far out in the dark. No single star was near enough to cast much light on the subject; the computer was enhancing galaxy shine and other background light to produce even this much image. Riker and Troi were in their seats, watching the screen; Worf was at his position, scanning attentively; and Data never took his eyes off the screen at all.

"Anything else showing on scan?" said Picard.

"Not a whisper," came Ileen's voice from *Marignano*. "The ion trail of the larger vessel leads away. Accelerating again. Heading for warp nine, by the looks of it."

"Blast!" Picard said. "The two ships can't have been in conjunction for very long."

"No more than two hours, I would estimate," said Data. "Approaching now."

"Do so with caution, Mr. Data," said Picard.

"At point-zero-one light-years," said Data. "Dropping out of warp."

"We're with you, *Enterprise,*" said Clif from *Oraidhe,* and the rainbow of deceleration sheened around her. Picard glanced over at the big, overengined shape and was glad of the sight. *Marignano* popped out of warp as well, and the three of them moved in together at the apexes of a triangle, running on impulse now but still decelerating.

Ahead of them *Boreal* drifted, moving on no more than inertia left over from whatever had grabbed it. The ship swelled in the viewscreen, the same cylinder they had seen not too long before, yawing very slightly and apparently unhurt. There were no burn marks, no decompression exits, no trace of anything that might be battle damage.

Not another Marie Celeste, Picard thought. "Life signs?" he said.

Worf studied his panel, checked it again, then shook his head and glanced at the captain with bemusement. "Showing better than four hundred humanoid life signs," he said. "That would closely match the predicted crew and passenger complement."

"Yes, it would. Hail them."

"Yes, sir." Worf worked at his console for a moment, frowning. "No answers to hail, Captain."

"They were a little resistant before," Ileen said.

"That is true," said Worf. "But at least last time there was active carrier. Now I hear nothing at all."

"Go to yellow alert," said Picard. The ship's sirens began hooting behind him. *"Marignano* and *Oraidhe,* assume defensive positions as briefed. We must assume that this may be a trap."

"Affirmative, *Enterprise."*

The three ships gathered around *Boreal* and matched course with it, dumping acceleration until they had matched its drift.

"Scans, please," said Picard. "Take your time."

There were a couple of minutes of silence, then Ileen's exec said, "Captain, we read what appear to be four hundred and twenty-eight life signs, all overtly normal, all within normal humanoid parameters."

Picard nodded slowly. *This is what I was afraid of. Much worse than a* Marie Celeste . . . *if I'm right. I much hope I'm dead wrong.*

"This is a little on the creepy side," Maisel said, almost too quietly for anyone else to hear. Then she turned to her exec. "Prepare two away teams—no, make it three. *Enterprise, Oraidhe,* I suggest you hold position. We'll take point on this one."

"Ileen," Picard said, "if I didn't know better, I would think that you were trying to hog all the excitement for yourself."

"Jean-Luc," the reply came at once, "fortunately you do know me better. And you know that what I want is you boys—and your big guns—at my back. If it came to the pinch, then of our three ships you know which one Starfleet would consider most expendable." She chuckled, a dry little sound. "That's why we're out here."

"Nonetheless," Picard said, "I'd like to send at least one team with yours."

"No argument there," she said.

"Let's have a schematic of *Boreal,*" Picard said to Data. It came up on the screen at once, alongside the image of the quietly drifting vessel.

"Got it," said Ileen. "I'll put my teams here—here—and here." Highlighted spots came up on the diagram. "Jean-Luc, how many teams? Clif?"

"Two for us," said Picard, hoping there were no surprises waiting for them on board *Boreal* that would make two teams insufficient.

In the transporter room, Riker looked over his team: Dr. Crusher and several security personnel. He touched his communicator. "Bridge, Riker. Anything new on scan?"

"Nothing, Commander," said Data's voice. "All is as before."

"Then let's get on with it. Energize."

The transporter room shimmered away from

around them, replaced in an eye blink by the open, parklike space in which Picard's team had walked. Phasers at the ready, they stood and looked around. There was no motion except for the artificially generated wind in the trees. No sound, no movement, just small, huddled lumps here and there in the grass on the artifical flooring.

People.

Crusher hurried over to the nearest one. It was a child, dressed in some kind of plain coverall, slumped on the ground with one small hand tucked, as if by accident, beneath a plump, pale cheek. The position was almost sleeplike, but the eyes were open.

Riker felt his stomach clench, as it always did when confronted with death. He knelt beside Crusher and watched, briefly useless, as she passed her medscanner over the body.

Except that it wasn't a body. The breath went in and out, its rhythm steady; the half-closed eyes gazed without flickering at something invisible off in the distance. But other than the respiration, there was no movement. There was no sign that the child had noticed them or registered their presence at all. Riker looked at Crusher.

She shook her head. "Autonomic brain activity," she said. "Nothing more. Nothing cortical." She looked up at the security people. "Fan out. See how many more are like this."

The team moved away, and Riker touched his communicator. *"Enterprise?"*

"Enterprise here," said Picard's voice. "What have you found?"

Riker stood up and looked around. "We're in your original beam-down point, Captain. There are a lot of people around who—if they're like the ones we're looking at right now—are deeply unconscious. Alive, but . . ." He glanced down at the little boy by his feet. "But not responsive."

"Enterprise away team," said Ileen Maisel's voice, "we've got a lot of unconscious people over here. We're working toward the command and control center, and it all looks very . . ." There was a silence, the unsound of someone hunting for words adequate to the situation. "Did I say spooky? I didn't say the half of it."

Dr. Crusher sat back on her heels, looking at the little boy, then tapped her own communicator. "Crusher to every away team," she said. "Medical personnel?"

"Jim Spencer over here, Beverly," said *Marignano*'s chief surgeon. "I've only had the chance to examine a few cases so far. I'm seeing profound unconsciousness and no reflex response."

"Babinski?" said Crusher.

There was a brief silence, then, "Negative Babinski," said Spencer. He sounded confused.

"God, that's strange," Crusher muttered.

The *Enterprise* away team made their way through the ship. Nearly everywhere they went, the story was the same. Twisted forms lay on the ground or slumped against the shells of buildings and temporary structures. Sometimes they were still half sitting, in positions that suggested they had been about to get up. But they could not do so now.

Riker watched Crusher go from colonist to colonist, each time standing up with that same concerned, perturbed look. The away teams from *Oraidhe* and *Marignano* kept searching, too, checking in with Riker and the *Enterprise* team every ten minutes or so.

Boreal was large, but not so large that the search took very long. Finally, Riker touched his communicator one last time and said, *"Enterprise?"*

"Go ahead, Number One."

"All four hundred twenty-eight colonists have been located and accounted for. They're all the same way: alive but unresponsive, uninjured except for some cases of minor trauma. We don't know how. No reaction to stimuli, otherwise in good health. But . . ."

"Dr. Crusher?" said Picard. "What's your analysis?"

She stood in one of the broad hallways that led out of the central core parkland area toward the ship's C&C. "Captain, if it's etiology you're looking for, I have none to offer. This I can say: except for differences in physiology, all the symptoms are very similar to those of the Alpheccan we picked up from the crippled pirate vessel. We'll need to do a more complete diagnostic on them, of course; but there's another problem. All these people are going to require total medical and nursing care. None of them can move. They don't even blink their eyes. *Everything* is going to have to be done for them. It's a good thing we're three ships together at the moment, because just the simple maintenance care for these people—until we can find out if there's anything we can do for them—would completely overwhelm my staff."

"If they need this much care," said Riker, "then it makes more sense to rig a group care area in one of the cargo spaces or a shuttle bay. I'll see to it."

"Do so, Number One," said Picard. "We'll start beaming the casualties aboard all three ships once accommodation space has been prepared."

"Captain," Dr. Crusher said, "bearing in mind the uncertainty of what's going on here, I would strongly suggest that everyone who beams back goes through the decontamination filter. Also, I would like a forensics team over here."

"Already on their way, Doctor," Riker said. "This whole scenario looks too much like a locked-room murder mystery. No murder, but plenty of mystery."

Crusher looked around at the unmoving bodies of the *Boreal* colonists who were being gathered together by various away team members and the medical staff who had already beamed over. "Mystery has its moments," she said, shaking her head. "But as for the rest of it, I'd say there might be some things that are a lot worse than murder."

* * *

Picard called a meeting of all three ships' department heads a few hours later, when the work of moving the *Boreal* colonists was finished. They gathered in one of the larger conference rooms, a very sober and concerned-looking group indeed.

"Status of *Boreal?*" Picard said.

"The ship is much as you found it when you visited, Captain," Data replied. "Data in its computers seem to have been unharmed, though in view of recent findings this evidence may be unreliable. It must be said, however, that so far the computer log throws very little light on what has happened here. Crewmen working in C&C or at other camera-supervised posts are seen sitting or standing at their duties, and then suddenly they slump down and become comatose, as we found them."

"Do any of the ship's records show any sign of the larger vessel?" asked Picard.

"No, sir," said Data, "and again this makes me suspect that the recordings are somehow being tampered with, practically at source."

Picard nodded. "Can we have a medical assessment, please?"

Crusher and Spencer, of *Oraidhe,* were sitting together with the doctor from *Marignano.* All three looked concerned and embarrassed.

Crusher began. "Our three medical teams have spent the past several hours in triage on the four hundred twenty-eight people we brought back. None of them is showing any higher cortical function at all, neither reaction to sensation nor even what we would regard as thought."

She shook her head. "Their brains are plainly mature. They show all the correct clinical signs of people who have led active and intelligent lives. Development is correct for age and somatype; children's brains show varying and correct states of growth, depth of sulcae, and other strictly physical signs, but those brains are not *working.*"

"It sounds as if you're saying that something has wiped these people's minds clean," said Picard.

Dr. Spencer sat back in his chair and sighed. "Captain, it seems that way. But we might be wrong. The problem is that, even now, when we talk about consciousness, we don't yet know where it *lives.* We've gone through a hundred different theories in the past two hundred years. There have been times when people thought that all thinking and memory were physically located in the brain, and of course some kinds of memory *are.* But by and large, those have nothing to do with personality. 'Located' memory tends to be limbic memory, closely tied to senses like smell. But the issue of consciousness, personality, *where* your knowledge of yourself might live . . . we still have no certain answer for that.

"And we're left here with a problem that reinforces, painfully, how little we know. *These* brains, *these* minds, *should be working.* The people on that ship should be walking around, or at least sitting up in bed, able to tell us what happened to them.

But nothing works, except for autonomic functions run by parts of the brain so primitive that it's sometimes difficult to kill them."

"Can they be helped?" asked Picard.

There was a long, long silence as the three doctors looked at one another. "Captain," Crusher said at last, "the only key we've been able to find to that question lies in the *Boreal* people's associational networks themselves—the networks a mind uses to transfer and store information inside itself. Though they may not be physically located, we *can* look at the physical connections the networks use for short-term function. We can't see exactly what information is held there, or in what condition, any more than we can see electricity in a wire—but if you hold the wire, you'll find out fast enough if there's a current running. What we know about these 'wires' in the people from *Boreal* is that many of them are showing some damage to their 'insulation,' the sheaths of the protein myelin that covers many of them. Some of those sheaths are showing an unusual kind of derangement, as if the molecules had been partially or completely dissociated by some discharge of force."

"Is there any physical effect that can produce such a reaction?"

"There are several," said Dr. Spencer. "But we can't find any indication that any have been used. However, the suggestion would seem to be that those networks are lost. In those with the worst damage—most of them, interestingly, are children—it seems plain that those brains will never again be able to work the way they did before all this happened. Whatever this was."

"What we have here," said Dr. Crusher, staring at the table, then looking up with her eyes flashing, "are four hundred and twenty-eight people who will have to be cared for for the rest of their lives. It is almost as if something left the hardware of their brains largely undamaged, but erased the software . . . their intelligence, their minds."

Everyone sat quiet around the table for a little while. "I wonder," said Data, as he worked at the small information console down at the end of the conference table, "whether *erased* is necessarily the correct word."

"What do you mean?"

"I had asked the computer to compile a series of excerpts from the *Boreal*'s computer logs and tapes, and any other outputs that might have been salient for the time period we are examining," Data said. "There were several odd outbursts from various crew members during the period of time when the *Boreal* might have been under attack. It is worth noting here, by the way, that there is no evidence of the larger vessel in any of *Boreal*'s tapes or logs. Apparently the colonists were taken quite by surprise. But these excerpts, as closely as I can determine, would seem to coincide with the earliest part of the time envelope at which the *Boreal* and the larger vessel would have met."

He touched a control and looked up at the

screen. Everyone followed his glance. They found themselves looking into *Boreal*'s C&C: a very plain, utilitarian place, screens and banks of controls and a few places to sit, but mostly people standing, almost all of them wearing the plain gray or beige coveralls of the sect. The camera did not move; people wandered back and forth through its ambit as they went about their business, murmuring a word to each other here and there: "Almost there." "What's the time check?" "Have you got that last set of readouts?"

Then, suddenly, almost outside the view of the camera, someone stopped. A young man, blond, sharp-faced, paused just at the fringe of the pickup, looking thoughtfully off into the middle distance— or so it seemed. He shook his head, and then slowly, slowly collapsed like a puppet with its strings cut. He folded down to the floor, lingered on his knees for a moment, then, loose-limbed, dropped the padd he had been carrying and simply fell over sideways. Some people at the table jumped slightly at the sound his head made as it struck the floor: Spencer nodded a little and looked at Crusher. "The compressed fracture I mentioned to you," he said.

There were soft sounds all around the pickup: things being dropped, something knocked off a console and clattering to the floor, and, again, soft sounds like heavy rolls of some material being thrown down. Not just material: bodies falling, slumping. And out of pickup, off to the right and out of view, a voice saying, loudly at first, "No— no, don't! Don't take that! Don't take that—it's my life! Don't take it, *don't take my life!*" and then fading. "Don't," the voice sobbed one last time, not as if in pain but in grief. And then another sound, heavy, another bolt of silk thrown on the floor . . .

Silence.

" 'Don't take it,' " Clif said, looking over at Ileen. " 'Don't take my life.' Not the body's life, then, but something more."

"Not erasure, then," Picard said, in a wondering voice, and a horrified one. "The removal of the life of the mind. Maybe of the mind itself? *Stolen?*"

The silence fell again. Finally, Picard said to Data, "I want you to continue with your analyses of anything from *Boreal*'s logs that would seem to cast light on this situation. What else is being done that we need to consider?"

Riker said, "The forensic team is continuing its work, Captain. We're going over that ship with a fine-tooth comb. Anything that our sensors can find . . . we'll have a report for you shortly."

"Very well. We cannot take *Boreal* with us," Picard said. "I think it would be best to quarantine this ship just as we did with the pirate vessel. What about the trail of the larger vessel?"

"It leads away quite clearly toward the galactic northeast," said Worf, "toward the pole. It does not appear to be making any attempt to hide its trail, or to be using cloaking devices."

"That," Ileen said, "gives me pause. It's plainly big and powerful enough not to care. And we've got to find it, catch it . . ."

"And possibly bring it to battle?" Picard said, looking grim. "Yes. But not until we fully understand exactly what it is we're dealing with here. Acting too soon can be as dangerous as not soon enough. And now we're left with another problem. What guarantee have we that what it's done to them it can't do to *us?*"

Silence again around the table. *"Boreal* was a little short on shielding of any kind, Captain," said Chief Engineer Geordi La Forge. *I* must *be distracted,* thought Picard. *I didn't even see him come in the room.* "Except what's normally associated with a ship that needs warp drive to move. If what we're seeing here is some kind of energy effect, we've had enough experience over time with tuning our own shields to keep such an effect out. But we have to know exactly what it is to block it, first. And I have to say, I don't know of any field that would produce the effect on people that we've seen on *Boreal.* Unless Dr. Crusher has some better idea."

"I have none," she said. "Believe me, I wish I did."

"So do we all, Doctor." Picard looked around the table. "Does anyone else have anything to add?"

No one did. "All right, then," he said. "Dismissed."

The room began to clear. The three captains, by tacit agreement, remained behind.

"Captain," said Maisel, "I hear you've got some nice holodeck programs over here. I could definitely use a run through one or two of them this evening. Everyone knows I'm a creature of the utmost composure, but after what we've just seen . . ." She shuddered.

"We're in agreement there," Picard said softly. "Clif?"

Clif looked up. "Oh, sorry, Captain, I missed that last—"

"You look a little distracted."

Clif shook his head. " 'Don't take my life,' " he whispered. "What could do a thing like that? Just steal a life, a mind, or an intelligence, suck it away—"

"There are creatures that live on, devour, the life force of others," Picard said. "Or there have been, anyway. Often enough, it hasn't been the devouring creature's own fault; is it *your* fault how your species has evolved? Not, I suppose, that that seems to matter much to the creatures the predator preys upon."

Ileen looked slightly grim at that. "To the sheep," she said, "the only good wolf is a dead wolf, I guess . . . despite everything the wolf knows about how social and intelligent its own culture is. And I doubt the situation changes as you progress up the food chain. Why should the weasel approve of the hawk that kills it, just because they're both predators?"

"Come on, Ileen," Clif said, standing up. "I can use a break myself, at the moment. Look, I'll take you out to dinner."

"Oh? What're you going to feed me?"

"A new delicacy I found out about," he said, and looked sidelong at Picard, "called hardtack."

"Sounds interesting," said Captain Maisel. "Let's go."

Picard sat quietly for a couple of moments, watching them go. Then he got up and took himself off to look for Beverly.

He found her in the cargo bay. It was normally a big, empty, cavernous, well-ordered place, all crates and containers stacked neatly, awaiting delivery or eventual use by people aboard ship. Everything had now been moved out, though, and instead Picard found himself looking at what closely resembled a field hospital.

He caught sight of Dr. Crusher about halfway across the huge room and slowly made his way across to her, stepping quietly between the rows of emergency mattresses that had been laid on the floor. On each one, wearing a coverall, lay a person. As Picard passed one of the mattresses, someone in an ensign's uniform came to its occupant—a young blond-haired woman—and turned her carefully from her right side onto her left. There was a horrible looseness about the way her arms moved, flopping over like a doll's, and for a moment, in the middle of the turn, vividly blue eyes stared, empty, up into lights the woman couldn't see. Her pupils contracted a bit, but nothing else moved.

Picard swallowed and made his way over to Beverly. She was holding her scanner over a tall, prone man whom Picard looked down at and recognized, with a slight shock, as the team leader; that face, animated if hostile, was now lying relaxed. And was that a twist of a smile? All very strange. All the rage gone, all the irony and cynicism that had lived in the face, all smoothed away. Picard didn't like the new expression at all.

Beverly looked up, nodded at Picard. "Is it anything urgent?" she said.

Picard shook his head. Dr. Crusher looked for a moment more at her medical tricorder, shut it, and looked all around the room, with an expression of helpless pain. "I don't know what we're going to do, Jean-Luc," she said, glancing at the rows and rows of people. "I really don't know."

After a moment she began to walk down one of the rows, looking at the floor, not at any of the people, and Picard went with her. "A long time ago," she said, "when I was just starting my training, they were taking us around to various facilities to show us the way various kinds of medical treatment were being implemented for people with different kinds of problems. I was"— she laughed at herself—"a pretty tough cookie, or I thought I was. They showed us all frightening things—things that really upset some of the other students—and they didn't bother me. I was kind of proud of that. Then, one day, they took us to a school for people with mental disabilities. Very young children, mostly. Some of them were well enough to ride around on little trikes or say a few words. Some of them weren't that well at all. *Most* of them weren't. There was a big playroom, and there were children there who simply stood against the wall—one or two who couldn't be stopped from repeatedly hitting the walls, so the walls, naturally, were soft. And there were a few who just stood, or sat, and looked. Looked out into space, didn't see anything, didn't hear you when you spoke to them. And it just hit me, suddenly, the waste of it all, the sheer waste. Here were children at the beginnings of their lives; they should have had everything to live for. Everything. But a misplaced gene, or a misdiagnosis *in utero,* or something else—in each of their cases something had gone wrong, something that not even our medicine could do anything about, not all our drugs and treatments and know-how would ever matter. Otherwise they wouldn't have been there. Calling the place a school was a dreadful misnomer, or whistling in the dark, at best. Certainly these children had committed professionals around them, doing everything possible to make them comfortable, giving them affection and good care ... but it would never matter. *None* of it would matter."

Crusher kept walking quietly. "And I broke

down," she said. "I cried for almost an hour—I just couldn't stop. They had to take me away and calm me down, and for the next couple of days I would just start crying again, without warning, at the memory of that place. All my instructors were worried about me. I couldn't explain to them that it was simply because, in that pretty, sunny building, I had seen the most horrible thing in the world. Human beings without the thing that makes them human, without *minds*. Creatures meant to be thinking beings. What's the line? 'A little less than the angels.' And there would never *be* anyone inside, no matter what we did."

She stopped, looked around slowly at the room, very quiet, then looked up at the captain. Her expression was as fierce with anger as the one a few seconds earlier had been fierce with grief. "Find what did this, Jean-Luc," she said. *"Find what did this* . . . and make it pay."

Quietly, as if not to wake the sleeping, Picard strode out of the cargo bay.

It was evening in the Caribbean. The rose and violet holodeck-generated sunset lay low on the horizon. There was no crew on deck; the sheets were down and reefed, and only two figures were to be seen, walking the deck more or less together: a tall blond man, a short curly-haired woman.

Picard went over to join them. As he came up with them, he noticed that Clif was shaking his shoulders oddly every few seconds. "I'm going to itch for a week now," he said.

Captain Maisel snickered. "Serves you right for trying to feed me that stuff."

She placed her hands on her hips in mock indignation as Picard joined them. *"You* set this up. He tried to feed me a piece of wood!"

"It was a biscuit," Clif said.

"It can't have been," Ileen said. "It had wood-worm. I *saw.*"

They all sat down together on the big steersman's bench at the stern and felt the ship rock and looked at the evening for a while. Ileen breathed deeply. "I love that salt air," she said. "Even though it makes me cough later."

"Dr. Crusher says it's a crude form of respiratory therapy," said Picard, "and the coughing is good for you." But he was aware of sounding a little absent as he said it.

"Jean-Luc," Captain Maisel said—and the look in her eye suddenly reminded him strongly of the look just worn by Beverly Crusher. "Do me a favor. If that happens to me, whatever that is, my release statement is on file with my crew, and with Star-fleet. Make sure it's enforced. I'd sooner be dead than like *that* . . . not long-term. Not even for a few months. There comes a time when, when you're gone, you should be let *go*. I won't be kept."

Picard sat quite still, sobered by the sudden intensity. He raised his eyebrows, glanced over at Clif. "And you, Captain?"

"Well . . ." He leaned back, looking not too concerned. "I have a similar release on file, but it's not likely to be needed. Should something happen to the symbiont, then the host won't last long. Should something happen to the host, the symbiont is probably dead anyway, either in the original accident or because this far out there's no way to get home in time to beat the transfer deadline to another host."

"I suppose," Picard said, "that's always a threat for your people when they go to space, especially deep space."

"Always," Clif said. "But some of us feel it's worth the risk, in terms of the enhanced experience we bring home to our people—if we were successful, anyway. And when you come right down to it, it's not much of a life without risk."

Ileen leaned over the rail, looking down at the swirl of light in the water. "The algae are restless tonight," she said, as a great curving whorl of green fire went by under the ship. "What was it they used to call it? 'Demon rum leaking out of Davy Jones's locker' or something like that?"

Picard burst out laughing. "Where do you hear these things? I think you make them up."

She shrugged. "Speaking of rum—"

Clif sighed and handed her a small flask he had been carrying. Ileen took a long, thoughtful drink, blinked, coughed in an evaluatory kind of way, and then coughed again and had another drink.

Picard and Clif looked at her, and she gazed calmly back at them. "After today," she said, "I think I can use it."

"Well," Clif said in a tone of good-natured scorn, "that's hardly the *worst* thing you've ever seen—"

"No," she said cheerfully enough. "I guess not. There was this floor show in the capital city in one of the countries on beta Ophiuchi Six, I can't remember its name, but I never thought I'd live to see a gelatin dessert perform a nautch dance. And in the middle of it, this guy comes out and starts singing—"

There was a whistle in the middle of the air. With some relief, Picard said, "Picard here—"

"Captain," said Data, "I have completed some of those correlations you were asking for, and I have come across some very disquieting results."

"I'll be right there."

"Sir, there is no need," Data said. "I can display them for you right there, if you like."

Picard glanced at Clif and Ileen. Ileen had put aside the rum bottle and looked interested. Clif nodded.

"Please do."

A hologrammatic simulation of a viewscreen appeared in the air, hanging over the deck of the ship and carefully slewing as the deck did. "I started," Data said, "by sampling for the most—"

"Oh, for gosh sakes, Mr. Data," said Captain Maisel suddenly, "have the thing hold still. I'm getting seasick here trying to watch it."

"My apologies, Captain." The screen steadied and showed a list of ship names and star names. "During the past three hundred fifty years, there have been some ninety colonization attempts in this general area. In fifty-nine of them, the ships or vessels setting out with intention to colonize successfully reached their intended planets. Fourteen of these did not reach their target planets due to accident or, in two or three cases, sabotage. Of the remaining seventeen, we have no record. But it is very much worth noticing that of the fifty-nine 'successfully' established colonies in this part of space, only nine remain viable."

The list on the screen vanished to show a section of the surface of a huge sphere. Nine colonies were all scattered along this pseudosurface.

"Mark the 'unsuccessful' colonies for us, would you, Mr. Data?" said Ileen.

A rash of small red lights appeared in the darkness above the section of pseudosphere.

"Can you shade them in color, say, red through violet, to demonstrate the time at which they failed or seemed to fail?" Clif said.

"Certainly, Captain." The reds changed color here and there. All three captains peered at the diagram.

"I think there seems to be a slight correlation," Ileen said, squinting a little. "It's easier to see if you let your eyes go unfocused." She tried a couple different degrees of squint. "But I have to admit, I'm not entirely sure I'm not seeing things."

"I do not believe you are, Captain Maisel. There are indications of a sort of pathway or trail of 'failed' enterprises in this area, proceeding forward through time, but at no point crossing that spherical boundary."

"How are you defining *failure,* Mr. Data?" said Picard.

"Either investigators could find no trace of the colonists or their vessel on or around the planet on which they intended to settle," Data said, "or the ships themselves were lost, or lost contact with: in which case the point of light marks that ship's last known position. In a seventy-year period, there were three separate colonization attempts—one making for B Hydri, one for twenty-two Ophiuchi, and one heading for three thirty-four Scorpii. Here is the planet of B Hydri to which the first group was heading."

A planet's image appeared on the screen in front of them. "And here is the second."

Clif's mouth dropped open.

"And the third."

Picard stared.

The images were all slightly different, some taken with slightly better equipment, some with worse. They showed different aspects of each planet from slightly different directions, polar caps expanded in one, contracted in another, the light falling differently from the nearby primary. But those spotty little seas, the huge continents—

"Mr. Data," Picard said slowly. "What is the probability that all those are the same planet?"

"Quite high, I would say, Captain. In the case of the first and third images, the probability rises to ninety-eight percent—part of the same continent is visible in both. There is some change in the polar caps, but it is negligible. Albedo and, in the last two, gravimetric information are nearly identical."

Ileen said softly. "But the stars—the primaries of those planets—*this* planet was seen circling—they're light-years and light-years apart! B Hydri is nearly a *kiloparsec* from—"

"Yes, Captain," Data said.

When you eliminate the impossible, Picard thought, paraphrasing in his shock, *then what's left must be the truth, no matter how crazy it sounds.* "Someone is moving this planet around," Picard said.

"And the ships that set course for it," Clif said, "are never heard from again . . ."

123

Chapter Five

PICARD'S DREAMS WERE HAUNTED by images of huge, lumbering, dark shapes coming between him and the stars, cutting off the light, looming close, and closer . . .

"Morning" found the alien vessel still kiloparsecs away, to judge by its trail, neither accelerating nor decelerating, but losing them because of difference in speed, and heading steadily up and out of the galactic plane. Picard stood behind Data's console and looked at the computer's projection of the vessel's course. "Not many star systems up that way," he said softly. "A lonely, dark place to be heading into."

He went and had his breakfast and then headed off for the largest of the conference rooms, where the science departments' meeting had started a little earlier than scheduled. The room was already buzzing with about thirty staff from all three ships. Maisel was there, talking animatedly with her exec and her science officer, and a minute or so after Picard entered, Clif arrived, with Data close behind him.

The three captains sat down, and people sorted themselves out around the big table. When they were ready, Picard said, "Thank you all for coming. I'll ask Mr. Data to bring you up to speed on the newest information we have to consider and then . . ." Picard spotted Ilene sitting across from him, chewing on her lower lip. Clearly she had something to say. Picard paused and looked at her expectantly.

"At the risk of ruining my well-deserved reputation for tact and forbearance," Ilene said. The soft chuckles of her crew filled the room momentarily then died down. "I don't think any of us needs much of an introduction. I think we can cut right to the chase here."

Picard cocked his head to the side, then smiled slightly. "Point well taken, Captain Maisel. Why don't you begin?"

There was quiet around the table for a moment. Finally Ilene spoke. "We have ships that vanish when they approach a certain planet. And we have that planet turning up orbiting at least three different stars. Mr. Data, is there anything in the scientific literature about planets moving from star to star?"

"Nothing at all, Captain," Data said, and of all those in the meeting, Picard suspected he was the only one who could read the profound disappointment behind the words. "I have examined it most thoroughly."

"So we're in legend country here," Clif said, thoughtfully. "Galactic urban myth."

Now Picard smiled a little, for unwittingly Clif had put his finger on the idea that had kept Picard up late the night before. "Myth, perhaps," Picard said, "but myth typically has a core of truth. And I'm wondering if it's possible that the historians or, more properly, the folklorists might be able to shed more light on this problem than the scientists can, at least to start with."

Some of the science staff looked at him quizzically. "There are species that have been in space a lot longer than any of ours have," Picard said. "Now, not all of them are willing to talk much to the younger races. A lot of older species have gotten out of the habit of communicating much with our 'generation,' either because of physiological and psychological differences or because they just don't particularly care about us." He smiled, a little ruefully. Picard still remembered with mild embarrassment the long, sonorous, melodic response from one ancient alien he had interviewed for what he considered an important research project; it had taken three weeks of computer time to translate and had finally turned out to mean "Run along, sonny, you bother me."

Picard shook himself out of his reverie and continued. "After absorbing the information Mr. Data turned up last night, I kept feeling as if the idea of moving planets was familiar somehow. I went through all the scientific records and couldn't find anything germane."

"So you looked into the folklore instead," Pickup said, with an expression that suggested she would be hitting herself repeatedly in the head if she were in private.

"There are *three* citations in the Thompson index," Picard said. "And two out of the three are native to this general area of space."

He gestured at the screen again. "That first citation is from a source on Twenty-nine Persei VI and dates back about a hundred years. It's a very brief reference to a story about a space traveler from an alien species—it doesn't say which one—who simply reports having landed on a planet that then started to move out of the system in which it was located. The alien then fell into a coma and died."

At that Dr. Crusher, who had been sitting quietly at one end of the conference table, glanced up but said nothing. "One commentator in the *Chrestomathie*," Picard said, "cross-referencing to this motif, remarked on the similarity of this story to some old medieval tales from Earth, about sailors who accidentally land on a whale, mistaking it for an island. The whale then dives, either killing the sailors or leaving them in the water and very confused."

"I just bet," Riker said under his breath.

"The third citation," Picard said, "tells of a moving planet full of 'evildoers' which was destroyed—though the word used is *killed*—by the Organians."

Ileen raised her eyebrows and whistled softly. *"There's* a weird one," she said. "Talk about ancient history. When's the last time we heard anything from them?"

"Quite a while back," Picard said. "We seem to have been left to get on with our business after their old prophecy came true, that one day we and the Klingons would be working together."

"So," Captain Maisel said, "the archetype, if that's what it is, has been heard of. Fine. But there are other things disturbing me. I keep hearing that guy's voice saying, 'Don't take my life, don't take it.' " She shook her head. "It gives me the creeps."

She was not alone: that voice had been haunting Picard last night as well. He leaned back to look out the conference room windows at the stars sliding by outside. "There," he said, "is exactly where the second citation comes in. Another piece of the puzzle . . . and maybe with everything else now on the table, it makes sense. I checked that citation very carefully last night. It comes from One Twenty-three Trianguli Three-A and Three-B—"

Clif looked at him. "The *Romulan* homeworlds?"

Picard nodded. "You do hear a lot of strange stories in a career in space," he said softly. "Way back in the *Stargazer* days, I heard this one in a bar after a meeting of an archaelogists' conference. It was very odd, so odd I made a note of it. Then, later, I found it more or less duplicated in a citation in the *Motif-Index*."

He turned back to the table again, folding his hands and studying them. "A lot of Romulan clans," he said, "have stories going back to the time when their parent species left Vulcan, or purporting to go that far back, anyway. *This* story says the ancestors of the Romulans left Vulcan in a fleet of seven pre-luminal 'generation' ships, having identified the One Twenty-three Tri system as a possible candidate for settlement along with several others. Their first couple of planetfalls turned out to be unsuitable for some reason or other, and they kept on going.

"At some point, though, the vanguard of the colonization fleet—the first three ships—were said to have come across a planet that seemed like exactly what they needed: climatically perfect, fertile, properly positioned around its sun. The first three ships that were traveling together were split regarding what to do about this, since the planet wasn't charted: the star had originally been reported barren. Some of the colonists didn't care about the apparently erroneous report—they seemed to be in favor of the whole fleet settling there. Other more suspicious colonists apparently felt that it was unwise to take a chance on the one planet's suitability. If they miscalculated, their entire splinter race might die out."

Picard sat back in his chair. "So, two of the ships decided to make planetfall there; the third continued to the next candidate star. When the fourth ship caught up with the first three, it found one of them gone, crashed on the planet surface, and another on its way down, its orbit rapidly decaying. Psi-talented communications crew on the late-arriving ship said they knew there were live minds on the ship that was going down, but there was no answer from any of them, only a horrible blankness. And something else they were supposed to have sensed: very strongly, and nearby, a great hunger recently assuaged. Then that ship crashed, as the first one had, hard: no question of any attempt at a soft landing. The ships *were* crashed, the story had it, purposely crashed by some agency of hunger."

Crusher looked up at Picard again at the mention of "blankness," and still said nothing. "The late-arriving ship stayed just long enough to assess the situation," Picard said, "conscious that their mechanical troubles must have saved them from the same tragedy. Whatever force had affected the other ships didn't affect them, and the crew of the late arrival wasn't minded to wait around until it did. They went on through the system as quickly as they could, on the trail of the other ship that hadn't lingered. The only colony ship that hadn't yet passed that way did so about a month later and found the star once again barren. There was no planet, and no sign remained of anything that had passed there. That last ship got out of there in a hurry and finally caught up with the vanguard, and the crews of those remaining ships settled the two Romulan worlds . . . so the story says."

Looks were exchanged around the table as Picard mentioned the missing planet. Picard turned again to look briefly out into the night. He could suddenly hear the voice of the man who had told him the story: rough, troubled, almost tormented. It might have been a long time ago, but some memories remained surprisingly sharp, almost as if they knew they would be needed someday.

Into the silence, Clif said, "We get little enough news from the Romulan homeworlds. And much of what we do hear is uncertain of provenance. You never know when you're being lied to for personal or political reasons, or just to keep the wicked aliens confused—"

Picard shook his head. "I think this material was trustworthy," he said. "At least, the man who told it to me believed it. Somewhat later I found, from other sources, that he was the son of a Romulan spy, and a spy himself, surgically altered; he looked as human as you do. He was then in fact mourning his father, who had just been killed, and he was in no mood to lie."

There was a silence. Pickup shook her head. "I don't know," she said. "It does sound like it could be a tall tale. After all, it might be embarrassing if word got out that your remote forebears fell foul of pirates, for example, after a navigational error. Much more interesting for them to be attacked by some kind of planet-moving, mind-eating monster . . ."

" 'Mind eater,' " Picard said somberly, "was very close indeed to the name the Romulan gave it: *iaehh,* 'Intellivore.' And, Lieutenant, I thought as you did, originally. But the Romulans' ancestors apparently knew pirates well enough, having lost at least one ship to them earlier, and my source had no hesitation about describing *that* encounter."

Ileen put her head in her hands briefly. "What exactly *is* this thing? Is it a species? Is it a single creature? Is it some kind of hive mind . . . or something else entirely? Or is the whole damn *planet* sentient, and it's just grown itself a warp drive? Or bought itself one."

"One thing makes sense," Dr. Crusher said suddenly. "If it is indeed an 'intellivore,' as the captain describes it—then that might explain why it bothers raiding ships when it has such power. It needs—or simply wants"—she made a helpless gesture—"maybe not mind itself. 'Intellivore' may be a misnomer. I doubt even a telepath could explain to me how mind itself is something you could *eat.* But something *associated* with mind— the ambient energy of living creatures' minds, maybe even their own sense of sentience—"

That thought had occurred to Picard, and it had

given him the shivers. He watched it do the same to Beverly now as she stopped, and shook her head. "This *is* legend country," Crusher said softly. "For pity's sake, it's the *boogeyman* we're talking about here. Things that jump at you out of the dark and eat your brains. *That* I could cope with! But *this*—"

"Doctor, I wouldn't instantly reject the concept out of hand," said Dr. Spencer from a little farther down the table. "There are some consciousness theorists who talk perfectly calmly about cognitive processes such as thought and memory producing transient nonphysical 'byproducts,' the way muscle use produces lactic acid in humans and its analogues in other hominid species. I'll grant you, when I've read some of these people's papers, I've wondered whether your brain eaters had been snacking on their authors." There was a soft chuckle around the table. "But now I'm beginning to wonder. There is still so *much* about mind that we don't know."

"And so much about our present problem," Riker said, frowning. "Captain Maisel's question is rather to the point. Somehow we have got to get more information about what this thing is, if we're going to assemble any kind of defense against it."

"If the captain's source's story is accurate," said Data slowly, "and the pre-Romulan colonists did indeed telepathically sense a 'hunger,' then perhaps there is some hope for us in the sort of telepathic screening technology with which the Vulcans have been experimenting. It remains in its earliest stages. They have been working on mechanical screening devices for young Vulcans in hormonal-surge telepathic overload, and so far there has not been much success, but—"

"—but *you* haven't been working on it, Mr. Data," Picard said, with just the slightest smile. "Perhaps you should look into it. For the time being, until we can assemble additional information—and additional theories—I would recommend that we keep our distance. But we will not be able to do so forever."

"Damn right we won't," said Captain Maisel. "Jean-Luc, we need to get at least close enough to confirm that what we're chasing is *that.*" She nodded at the viewscreen, which was still showing the multiple images. "We don't have to do it ourselves; we can send a probe."

"The only difficulty there, Captain," said Data, "is the possibility that the intellivore—if indeed that is what we are now pursuing—will tamper with the probe's memory as soon as it detects it, causing it to show us whatever illusion it pleases. Perhaps mere empty space, or a large alien vessel?"

Ileen frowned at the table. "I *hate* this thing," she muttered. "What this is going to do to my research schedule!"

"Mr. Data," Picard said, "perhaps you had better get started as quickly as possible on the telepathic-screening end of this problem. If you can devise some kind of shield for the probe, however crude—enough to let us get a safe look at what we're pursuing—it will certainly reduce the number of unanswered questions by one."

"It may increase the number of problems by one as well," Clif said suddenly. "Captain, if the intellivore is indeed a creature that lives by, or *on* minds, and it can sense thought, then it stands to reason that it may very well be able to sense the blockage of it . . . and where more subtle weapons fail, it may have *less* subtle ones to fall back on. Have you thought about the kind of weaponry you could hook into a warp drive big enough to move a planet?"

Picard had thought about it. He grimaced and shook his head. "It doesn't matter. We have to start somewhere. We'll maintain our distance until we're ready to take a closer look; then we'll make further plans."

Picard rose. "Meanwhile, the rest of you will want to go over this information in more detail. If there's any light you can shed on the work Mr. Data will be starting, please do so—and don't ignore any possibility, no matter how unlikely it seems. I'd like to see a written report and discussion of the topics we've been working on within a few hours."

Picard spent the next few hours in his ready room, taking care of "housekeeping"—the kind of ship's business that always tends to pile up during busy periods.

It was an escape, and he knew it. Those empty mats on the floor of the cargo bay, the quiet, somehow accusing look in Crusher's eyes—those were beginning to haunt him.

When he came out of the ready room, he found that Data was missing from the bridge, and Troi as well. "They're down in engineering, Captain," said Riker, heading to Data's console to look over the shoulder of the officer manning it, keeping an eye on their course. "Data's building the probe."

"Already?" Picard said.

Riker gave him a wry look. "You know Data. Wave a new theoretical problem in front of him, and stand back! But he had some help. He and Deanna came in here together talking a mile a minute after the meeting broke up, and they went out again talking faster."

A couple of hours later, the combined science staffs' report was waiting for Picard on the bridge. The word *conjecture* was all over it: it was full of disclaimers and hedgings, and it raised the hair on the back of his neck, regardless.

The picture it drew was one of a long history of terror in this dark fringe at the edge of the galaxy. There were more references to planets that traveled, planets that killed, in the *Chrestomathie*. Some of them were in the records of the oldest races. They seemed to indicate that this phenomenon had been occurring, on and off, for certainly hundreds of years, possibly more like thousands.

Some of them were probably just stories; some were almost certainly caused by the intellivore.

That name, the translation of the Romulan word, had stuck in the report. Here, too, some of the references were unsubstantiated legends, and some of them were true. The interesting thing about the true stories was that all such life-eating species had been wiped out a long time ago—or at least had managed to "never be seen or heard of again." One of the *Oraidhe* science staff suggested that at least one of these vanishings might not be genuine, that perhaps one species somewhere decided to find itself a lifestyle that was a little more mobile, probably after repeated attacks on it.

Picard shifted uncomfortably in his chair and reflected on this enormous source of power that had not been used to its full potential. If the intellivore planet or species was a predator, it was a somewhat passive one, or, at least, it seemed to have been so for most of its history. It would more or less tiptoe out of the darkness, slip into orbit around some star, and wait for orbital mechanics in the area to calm down. There it would linger, waiting for travelers, for colonists . . . and it waited in places that suggested it knew people were coming. If it was responsible for tampering with the *Enterprise* probe, that was probably a good example of its preferred modus operandi. It would discover who was coming, be there ready for them, and when they arrived, it would suck their lives dry.

In the middle of reading the report, Picard had to stop, go into his ready room, and get himself a cup of tea. For a while, he stood across the room, gazing at his desk and the screen on it.

Finally, he put the teacup down and strode decisively toward his desk. It was time to finish studying the information so he could begin to act upon it.

"Recommendations are as follows," the last page began. "Positive identification." Well, that would come soon enough, Picard hoped, when Data sent another probe out.

"Once identification is complete, closer examination and further evaluation."

"Oh, wonderful," Picard said under his breath. "Who gets to bell the cat?" And almost instantly, in his mind, he could hear Captain Maisel offering to do it—insisting on it, in fact. He rubbed his eyes and smiled bitterly, wondering which would sap his energy faster, a face-off with the creature or a face-off with Ileen. *Never a dull moment.* He shifted his eyes back to the padd.

"Then contact, if possible. If so, translation, establishment of common context, and discussion."

Supposing it *did* communicate with them; that would open a whole new kettle of worms, as he had heard Riker say once. This part of space had been relatively unpopulated for a long time. The intellivore might see all these colonists as an invasion force, something to be defended against. Possibly it was even a weapon itself, another doomsday machine, raised, built, or made for this purpose. It couldn't be blamed for such.

Or alternately, it might not be able to communicate, or willing to. Further, it might attack them. They would resist.

And the question is . . . with what?

After that, the report suggested merely "implementation." Acting on whatever solution had been worked out. Assuming that one could be.

Chapter Six

SEVERAL HOURS LATER, anyone with any excuse to be on the bridge was there. Data sat at his station, running last-minute checks on the probe. To Picard's eye, he looked almost nervous. He seemed to be taking unusual care over the business of checking and rechecking the status of the probe's screening.

"I trust the probe will launch on time, Mr. Data," Picard said in a more impatient tone than he had intended.

"Forty-five seconds now, Captain."

They seemed to stretch. Data kept working at his panel. Troi, sitting at Picard's left hand, raised her eyebrows, and Picard said quietly to her, "I don't suppose you've sensed anything significant during these close brushes with the intellivore—assuming that's what it is?"

Troi shook her head as she replied, "It's very difficult to get any kind of reading on another mind moving at this speed. But I'm hoping I'll sense something as we start to catch up."

Picard nodded. "The *instant* you notice anything—"

"Believe me, Captain, you'll be the second to know."

"Probe launched," Data said.

On the screen, they watched the line of light arc away from the *Enterprise* into the darkness, and forward into the starfield sliding by.

"How long to optimum approach?" Picard asked.

"At present speed, fifty-seven minutes, Captain."

"Very well."

They waited. Bridge crew went about their business; others came in and out, but never stayed out for long. At about forty-nine minutes, Picard said to Worf, "Are *Oraidhe* and *Marignano* on the line?"

"With us, Captain, and watching."

"Any comments, Captain Clif? Captain Maisel?"

"Just waiting for the data," Maisel said.

Clif said, "Yes. Somehow I don't feel compelled to go off and catch up on my reading just now . . ."

"Standing by," Picard said.

They waited. "Three minutes," said Data.

"Probe status?" Riker said.

"Communications are nominal. I will be shutting down our direct comm link to the probe in the next fifty seconds."

"Shutting it down *now?*" Riker said, glancing at the captain.

"I do not wish to take the chance of an active trace directly back to our comm systems, and possibly to our computer."

Picard nodded. "At your discretion, Mr. Data."

After what seemed a very short time, Data said, "I have closed down comms. Contact with the object in approximately one minute."

Everyone looked at the dark screen, as if it could be made to give up its secrets by staring. Picard resisted the urge to go into his ready room and pace.

"The probe should be in sensor contact with the vessel now," Data said. "Preprogramming will hold its sensor window open for another four minutes. Then it will close."

"Any change in the velocity of the vessel?"

"None, Captain. It appears unaware."

Let's hope it really is, Picard thought.

Seconds ticked by. Picard found himself listening to his own heartbeat to time them. Finally, "Sensor window closing," Data said. "The probe will be establishing contact shortly."

Silence. They all waited . . .

"Contact reestablished," Data said.

The silence on the bridge was complete. People

stared at the viewscreen, and an image flashed into being there.

It was a planet, about twice the size of Earth, seen as if illuminated by strong starlight from one side. The patterns of the continents, the shapes of the oceans, the ragged shape of the icecap, which was centered on the planet like the boss of a shield, facing toward them as it leaned into its course away from them—all of them were familiar.

"Identification is verified," said Data. "This is the planet that was associated with the colonization efforts whose disappearances we have been investigating."

Picard sat quiet for a moment, then almost whispered, *"Marignano?"*

"Acknowledged, Captain," said Ileen, and there was a strange sound of enjoyment in her voice. "There it is . . ."

"Yes, and we'll discuss it in a while. *Oraidhe?"*

"I see it, Captain," said Clif, and there was a sigh. "Z-eight-zero-eight-zero-point-four . . ."

"So it would seem," Picard said. "Another one for the books."

Picard found Beverly in her office in sickbay, looking rather worn, enough so that she didn't rise to greet him when he came in but simply gestured with her eyes at the seat nearest her desk. "Jean-Luc—" she said.

He sat down, looked at her. "How are you holding up?"

"Oh, as well as can be expected under the circumstances. I'm doing counseling with my staff, they're doing counseling with me. None of us much likes the kind of care we're having to deal with at the moment. However, we're coping."

"Any improvement in any of your patients?"

She gave him a rather bitter look. "Some of my staff have voiced the opinion that the only improvement likely for any of these people is—" She broke off. "Well. The one that in many cases we can't give them."

"Some of them had release documentation on file in *Boreal*, then?"

"A very few of them. Not nearly enough. Those we can let go, we will . . . but . . ." She shook her head. "Never mind. You're here about something else." Before Picard had a chance to reply, the doctor turned to her desk screen and tapped at it for a moment. "The first vessel we found," she said, "the pirate vessel with everybody missing except the Alpheccan left on board—"

"Do we have any indication of where those people went?"

"Not that I know of, Captain. However, the forensics team went over the outer hull as well as the inner—normal technique. They found something that didn't strike me as particularly significant, early on. These."

She turned the screen so that he could look at it. Picard found himself examining a wire-frame structure that looked more like a beach ball or soccer ball than anything else. "Why does this look familiar?" he said.

Beverly smiled a little. "It's a buckyball."

"Pardon?"

"A buckminsterfullerene. It's a dodecahedral solid, an arrangement of carbon atoms into a somewhat spherical lattice. It was named after Buckminster Fuller, an Earth scientist and architect who worked with geodesic spheres based on a similar structure. For a long time they were thought only to be artificial: they had industrial uses, and people learned how to make them under very specific requirements of heat and pressure. But then it was discovered that they could occur naturally, and that often, inside that latticework, other atoms, sometimes quite old ones and from sources very different from the original fullerene, could be trapped for long periods—held, as it were, in a kind of molecular stasis and protected from interacting with other compounds in their environment."

"A sort of cage," Picard said, "or collector's box."

"That's right. And a couple centuries ago, on Earth anyway, came the first detections of fullerenes in impact craters from meteorites and comet fragments. The fullerenes created during those impacts sometimes trapped atoms from the original cometary material inside their lattice structures, so that when you took the fullerene apart, inside it you would have a little piece of that original cometary material. Very useful for research, as you might imagine."

Crusher sat back in her chair. "Well. When the forensics team was done sweeping the pirate vessel, there was a fairly high incidence of fullerenes found on its hull. Now, I didn't make anything of that at the time. You can pick up that kind of debris by passing through asteroid fields where there have been a lot of random impacts, or just by traveling through particularly dusty areas of space, regions with a lot of dark matter.

"Then, of course, they found *Boreal.* I didn't have time to look at the forensics on *Boreal* for some time, as you might imagine. I had a chance to look at them yesterday morning. And I found a significant occurrence of fullerenes."

"Matching what you would have found on the pirate vessel?" Picard said.

"Somewhat higher. Difficult to say why, in this particular case, but they do match the fullerenes I found on the Alpheccan's vessel."

Picard sat quietly for a moment and then said, "It's still not quite conclusive, is it? If the two ships had passed through the same area of space, they could have picked up the same kind of debris—"

"Yes, but I would have expected a closer agreement on the 'background level,'" Crusher said.

And then she pushed the screen aside, and said, "Jean-Luc, why is it so hard for you to believe it?"

He looked at her.

"That thing out there, that planet—the intellivore—that's what made those pirates vanish and left that poor Alpheccan in the condition we found him. That's what reduced the *Boreal* people to the state they're in now. Why won't you believe it?"

"Beverly," he said, "in this particular area, belief is not my job. My job is finding out what happened, and I have to be careful to put aside my own desire to find a quick conclusion, which, believe me, I want as much as you do."

She looked at him, shook her head slowly. "That thing has already ended two hundred people's lives, and it's going to end many more if someone doesn't *do* something about it!"

"We don't have sufficient evidence to confirm that conclusion, Doctor," Picard said softly. "I will not act until I have something that will 'stand up in court.'"

"Captain," Dr. Crusher said, just as softly. "This thing takes beings, *any* beings, and sucks out of them the one thing that makes them people. Surely you can't intend to treat this"—she let out a long breath, looking for the right word—"this predator, this extremely clever and sophisticated predator, with the same consideration you would give to a human."

"Indeed I do not," Picard said, "because it is *not* human. It's my responsibility to remember that, and to treat it accordingly." Crusher stared at Picard for a moment, and then averted her eyes. "Was there something else, Doctor?"

She paused and shook her head slowly. "Jean-

Luc, I never thought I'd say this, but I think . . ." her voice trailed off.

"Go on," Picard said.

"I think you should *destroy it.* Before it does any more harm, eats any more lives, any more minds— kill it *now,* while you have a chance."

Picard sat silent for a few moments. "Your concerns are noted, Doctor," he said.

"I'm honestly not interested in being right, Jean-Luc," she said as he got up. "I'm just interested in preserving life. Life in its proper sense—not this half-life." She gestured with her head in the direction of the cargo bay, some decks down, some decks back. "I don't want any more patients like that. I don't want doctors on other planets to have any more patients like that. Please, sir . . . do what you can."

Picard nodded. Dr. Crusher turned away, looking at the fullerene rotating, planetlike, on her screen. Troubled, Picard went out.

He went to the meeting with Maisel and Clif almost with a sense of relief. Ileen and her exec were waiting for him already. Clif came in with his own XO a few minutes later.

"Well," Picard said finally, when everyone was settled, "I'm open to discussion. We have a problem."

They looked at the image of the planet, sailing away through the night, starlit. Ileen had augmented the image so that the contours of the warpfield around the planet were visible. It was huge, and of tremendous power: a great globe surrounding the planet, slightly compressed on the forward edge, narrowing to a whiplike tail behind, where the field sealed itself.

"You wouldn't want to blunder through that," she said absently, but with some relish. "If you hit the rear of it, it would cut you in half. *Look* at that symmetry! It's bizarre."

"It certainly doesn't match anything our science would accept as normal for a functioning warpfield," said Riker. "These people could teach us something."

"That's what I've been thinking," Captain Maisel said. "Captain, we should start a more aggressive series of sensor runs. This one seems to have been fairly successful, but the amount of equipment the probe could carry was limited. I think it's time a science vessel sees what it can find out, with all its eyes and ears peeled."

Picard had been waiting for this. He nodded, looked thoughtful, and said, "Clif?"

The Trill shook his head. "I have to disagree. We might have things to learn from that technology, but we're in danger of learning them the way the boy learned how rocks fall, by having one fall on his head. Hostile or not, even if it has the best of intentions—which some of us will question—that thing could possibly destroy us even in the act of doing something so seemingly innocent as trying to probe us in return. I think we need to sit tight for the moment, following it as distantly as possible. Be very careful not to attract its attention, and call for backup."

Picard blinked at that. "What kind of backup?" he said. "You know as well as I that we're supposed to be the front line in this situation. Three starships of the line: *we're* meant to handle this."

"We're going to lose time, Clif," Captain Maisel said. "And our opportunity, if we don't move quickly. Suppose that while we're being overcautious, this thing takes fright and runs off somewhere faster than we can follow. If we let this planet, or creature, or creatures, just waltz away from us now because some of us are too cautious to move when the happy opportunity presents itself, Starfleet is not going to be pleased!"

Cliff compressed his lips, then replied slowly. "There are twenty-five hundred Starfleet personnel out here, not to mention the two hundred casualties from *Boreal,* to whom we have a responsibility to get them back safely to where they can be properly cared for."

"If we don't move pretty fast now," Ileen said, "there are going to be a whole lot more people who need to be 'properly cared for'! At least that's the way I read how things are going. You look at Mr. Data's figures!" She got up and started to pace. "We need to do something *now,* and the something is going to have to take one of two forms. Either figure out a way to communicate with the planet, and explain to it or them the error of their ways, so to speak—or kill it. But one way or another, we're going to need more information to do that—and lying low is not going to solve the problem."

"I think Captain Maisel is right in this," Picard said. He looked at Clif. "I don't really see any virtue in calling for assistance. We were sent here to handle this ourselves. We're not in any immediate danger, as I judge it. Obviously, we'll give Starfleet as much information as we can about what's going on here. But for the time being, I think our best course is to continue doing what we're doing at the moment. We'll continue to tail the planet, close enough not to lose the trail. But I will assure myself of our own task force's safety before we go any further in actually engaging the creature or creatures."

There was a longish silence. "Captain," Clif said, "I wish you would think again about this."

Maisel let out a long breath of exasperation. "Your problem," she said, "is that you *like* that thing."

"I beg your pardon?"

"If the evidence is correct, if it does indeed live on other beings' life force . . ." She had the grace to look embarrassed. "Clif, I'm sorry, but I can see how you might empathize with it."

He gave her a slightly shocked look, then shrugged, smiled a bit. "Meaning that a Trill's form of parasitism might be more benevolent, but it's still parasitism? Just not one that destroys the host, or the other species needed to survive?"

"Well, I wouldn't have put it quite that way . . ."

"No, you let me do that." From anyone else, the statement would have been fairly cutting. But Clif just shook his head. "Captain Maisel, evolution is a strange thing. Here I am, something that, if history on Trill hadn't taken a strange turn or two, would have spent its life in a silt pool, in very nice telepathic contact with its own kind but no one else. Limited, constrained to one world, unable to leave it. Then something happened—the evolutionary twist that made it possible for us to 'parasitize.' And certainly our own history is obscure enough about the earliest forms of that relationship. There are stories of barbarities, exploitation, cruelty. Fortunately, we grew past the point where our bad habits could have killed us, as has happened to so many species here and there. And the host species came along—" Picard saw the odd smile on Clif's face. "We were lucky. If some more powerful species had come along and seen our earliest host-client relationships, and had decided that they were immoral, and wiped us out . . . we would never have had a chance to experience what I'm experiencing now. To travel the stars, to meet other beings . . . do wonderful things."

"History is full of these turnings," Ileen said. "But the kind of relationship that a Trill would have with its host is completely different in nature from the kind of relationship that *that* thing has with what it feeds on. Whether it actually ingests mind or intelligence or it's after something else, it doesn't really matter; the effect is the same. We've got to come to grips with it, either through communication and dialogue or through investigation that will lead us to a way to keep it out of our spaces and away from intelligent species. Let it go off somewhere else and graze, if it must . . ."

"I would find the morality of that rather questionable," Clif said gently. "Just because the drainings aren't happening in your backyard, then it's all right?"

She threw him an annoyed look. Then, "I think you're making a mistake, Captain," Maisel said to Picard.

Clif looked at him sadly. "So do I."

"Someone has to make the call," said Picard. "On this mission, I fear it's 'my turn in the barrel.' Another time, another place, it'll be one of you." He shook his head, looked at them both affably. "I intend to have my turn at thinking one of you is mistaken. That's why I make the choice I make now."

He fell silent. A captain did not usually dismiss other captains, even when senior and in command. Ileen and Clif got up; Clif was smiling a little ruefully.

"Well," he said, "I'll have a little more time yet for the holodeck, I suppose. Will you come over to *Oraidhe* and see ours?"

Picard nodded. "A little later," he said, "certainly."

"Give me a call when you're ready."

The two captains and their execs left, leaving Picard and Riker looking at each other.

"It's a hard call," Riker said.

Picard breathed out, more a hiss than a sigh. "For the moment, I see no other way to proceed."

Picard was awakened at the equivalent of three in the morning by Data's voice calling him to the bridge.

Picard sat up in bed, rubbing his eyes. "Lights, low. What is it?"

"Oraidhe has pulled ahead of the task force and is accelerating toward warp nine."

"I'll be right up."

He paused only long enough to throw last night's uniform on again, then headed up to the bridge at best speed. Riker was ahead of him, looking nearly as raggedy and tired as Picard felt, and talking to Captain Maisel. "Not a word to us, either," she said. "He just took off like a bat out of hell—"

"He is continuing to accelerate," Data said. "Approaching warp nine-point-four now."

"Hail him!" Picard said to comms.

"We've been doing so, sir," said the officer manning Worf's post. "Nonstop. No response."

"Did he just jump? Just like that?"

"No, Captain," said Data. "Our arrangement has been that any ship in the task force may move around discretionarily in about a one-light-year radius, as long as we all remain in communication.

Captain Clif had moved out to the border of that radius, had held there for a time, and then . . ."

"I'm going after him," Maisel said.

"Captain," Picard said, "I countermand you. You may not pursue. Hold your position!"

"Jean-Luc, it's got him!"

"If it has," Picard said, "you must not rush after it and give it a chance to get you, too."

There was a silence punctuated only by the sound of beeping monitors on the captains' respective bridges. "Mr. Data, what's he doing?"

"Holding at nine-point-four, Captain. He will catch up with the planet in approximately twelve minutes, at this rate."

Puzzlement compounded concern as Picard recalled running into Clif the evening before in Ten-Forward. Despite his earlier opposition, the Trill seemed to have accepted Picard's decision to wait and watch. In fact, Picard had even gotten a definite invitation to try the *Oraidhe*'s holodeck.

The captain of the *Enterprise* clearly remembered the gleam in his new friend's eyes as he asked Picard to join him for a mountain-climbing expedition he had just programmed. Picard never would have guessed that Clif was about to bolt.

"What's the planet doing?"

"It is decelerating, Captain—rapidly. Shortly they will have matched velocities, in less than three and a half minutes, if *Oraidhe* does not change its course."

Picard found himself keeping time by his pulse again, but he was having to divide by two. *Clif!*

But there was nothing to be done.

"Long-range scan indicates that *Oraidhe* will be within orbital range of the planet within one minute, Captain. Planet is matching."

They waited. "Captain," Riker said.

"No change of course," said Picard, grim. "Maintain speed and heading. Mr. Data, you said that you were evaluating their last log entry. What does it show?"

"This, Captain." Data touched the controls. The screen came alive and showed them *Oraidhe*'s bridge. Clif was there, looking over the shoulder of his own conn officer, saying, "They did *what?*"

"She's moving out, Captain. Look! Warp eight— warp nine—"

"My gods," Clif said, "they've got her. Go after them!"

"Captain!" said Clif's exec.

"They need our help," Clif said. "Go after them."

"What were they seeing?" said Picard.

"This, Captain," Data said. "The feed from their logs." He touched another control.

An image of the *Enterprise*, fleeing into the night, faster and faster—

"Warp nine. Nine-point-one. Nine-point-two—" said *Oraidhe*'s exec.

"Match," said Clif. "Catch them!"

Picard opened his mouth and closed it again, sat

down in his command chair, and gripped the arms of it.

"Decelerating now, Captain. Long-range scan shows them matching course and speed with the planet."

The bridge crew stared at one another with frozen and horrified looks. "Hold our present course," said Picard softly. "No change."

There was a long silence. Finally, Data said, *"Oraidhe* has dropped into normal space, Captain. On impulse, and decelerating. The planet is accelerating once more. Warp three—warp five—"

"Hold our course, Mr. Data," said Picard. "Wait until the planet has reestablished its lead. Comms, continue hailing *Oraidhe.* We will catch up with her." Picard looked around at the bridge crew. "As if nothing had happened. *Marignano,* do you copy?"

There was a sigh from the other end, angry and resigned. "I understand you, *Enterprise,"* Captain Maisel said, "and will comply." And she broke off.

They knew what they would find when they caught up with *Oraidhe.* Finding it only made it worse. The away teams beamed aboard, and found *Oraidhe*'s crew sitting at their posts, lying near them, slumped against walls—breathing, warm, only a few injured, no one dead . . . except in the way that counted most.

They found Clif sitting in his command chair, as they had seen him last: braced, hunched forward, fingers interlaced, now leaning quite far forward, like a man who had fallen asleep in his seat. Riker gently lifted the captain up, looked him in the eye. His eyes were open, but there was no one behind them. Everyone else—his exec, his science officers —families, children—all were silent, eyes empty, having seen what they could not tell, and now would never be able to.

Much later, Picard sat in his own command chair, his own bridge crew silent around him. He did not want to go near sickbay just now, knowing who would be there, and what she would be thinking.

And emphatically he did not want to go down to the holodeck and sit under a Caribbean sunset. The voice that had told him two beings' worth of terrible jokes under that sunset would not be speaking to anyone again, except in memory.

He looked at the starry dark—the stars sparse here, sliding away past *Enterprise* as she continued slowly on the course after the planet. He had ordered that they drop back a little—not far enough to lose the planet, but just a little. *Oraidhe* was on tow, on tractor beams; the slowing up was reasonable enough.

Picard looked into the emptiness. *This will not happen again,* he thought. *I swear it won't.*

But all around him he heard the echo of an oath that he might not be able to keep.

Chapter Seven

THE COMMAND CREWS of *Enterprise* and *Marignano* met again in the morning. To say that the mood was somber would be putting it mildly.

"It was a message," Maisel said, "what happened to *Oraidhe*. That creature out there has been in this business for a long time. It considers itself a match for us . . . and it's daring us to do our worst."

She paused and smiled, not a pleasant look. "We're going to have to," she said, "if we're going to survive."

Ruefully, Picard said, "I agree with you. It knows, I think, that we're locked into this pursuit . . . though whether it understands the reasons, I have no idea. It knows that sooner or later, it will have its opportunity to come at each of us."

"Why hasn't it done so now?" Riker said.

Data looked up. "I would conjecture," he said, "that it may be gorged. This is a bigger 'feed' than it, or they, have had since *Boreal* or the pirate vessel previous. I would suspect we have a little time."

"We're going to have to make best use of that time, then," Picard said. "Let me be clear: I am still open to the possibility of communicating with this creature or creatures, even now. We cannot forget our mandate, which is contact with new life. If that contact proves to be inevitably fatal, that's one thing; but the inevitability is not yet proven, and we must keep the option open if there's any way we can."

"I hear what you're saying, Captain," said Maisel, "but I think you're wasting your time. I think we had better postulate worst case."

Picard rested his chin on one hand and stared thoughtfully at Maisel. "All right. Though I'd prefer to see this resolved some other way, I agree we must postulate worst case. We must turn our minds to a way to destroy this creature or creatures, if it cannot be stopped otherwise. And we must act in ways that will encourage it to return to its more normal modus operandi."

"You're saying we should back off the chase?" said Ileen.

"If there were a way to cause it to think that we weren't even now interested in chasing it," Picard said, "possibly a way to lay a false trail—I would do that."

"There's something else we should be thinking about, Captain," said Riker. "The question of communication. From the evidence we have, the intellivore plainly understands our forms of communication well enough to read them. It can tell when ships and colonists are coming its way. Its translation facilities must be fairly well developed. All it should take would be one message in the clear, stating our intentions clearly, and then we can watch what it does. If it backs off, that's great. Or if it returns a communication in a reasonable time, then we can start working out what it wants to do."

That was true enough. "Meanwhile," Picard said, "the worst case. What do we know about this creature that will give us a way to attack it?"

There was a little silence. "It's a planet," Geordi said, a little reluctantly. "Planets have been blown up before."

"With planet-cracker bombs, yes," said Captain Maisel, rather dryly. "You have any on hand? They're not exactly Starfleet issue."

Geordi shook his head. "We don't usually carry such things, Captain . . . and I wouldn't care to be working in a Starfleet where we did. But, as usual with weapons of mass destruction as opposed to more useful and beneficial devices, they're not that hard to build."

Maisel blinked. "You have the materials?"

161

"We've got plenty of antimatter," Geordi said.

"Fine," said Picard, though he would normally not have described as "fine" any conversation in which he was discussing the purposeful destruction of a planet. "Still, as you say, if we're going to destroy this planet, we must know where to put the device. We'll need a much better scan of the planet's structure."

"*Now,* then," said Ileen.

"Please hold that thought, Captain," said Picard, desperately hoping that she would lose it. "We still have to consider the possibility of other weaknesses. Is there anything else we should take into consideration?"

Ileen finally cut through the long silence that followed. "We've got this cat," she said softly, "and this bell—"

Picard waited almost impatiently for her to volunteer. She just looked at him. "Captain Picard," she said, "I'm not suicidal, and this would be suicide. At least in terms of *this* death." She tapped her head. "This is the kind of situation where you call for volunteers, yes. But Starfleet has strong feelings about the captains of starships doing such things themselves."

"Yes," Picard said, "so it does." He gazed down at his folded hands, not quite willing to look at any of the people gathered around the table.

"We are, I suppose," said Ileen's executive officer, Commander McGrady, "talking about two shuttlecraft equipped with, or towing, the necessary shield generators, and another carrying the bomb—"

Data shook his head. "I do not think that is likely to be effective, Commander. In particular, the power level needed to drive the shields will need a starship."

"It would seem," Picard said, "we may be faced with the necessity of sacrificing one starship, or losing two as the price of a failed attempt."

"We have a spare," Ileen said very reluctantly.

Picard sighed. The crew complement of *Oraidhe* were in the process of being split between *Enterprise*'s and *Marignano*'s facilities, and the medical staff were complaining even more bitterly of the overload than they had been earlier. It was understandable, since their problem was now multiplied by approximately six. "We do," Picard said, "but, Captain, the intellivore knows it's already dealt with the crew of *Oraidhe*. I don't think it would hold still if that ship approached it again. I think it would leave quickly. Wouldn't you, in its position?"

"I don't want to think about its position . . . though I suppose you have a point."

"No," Picard said. "It's going to be your ship or mine."

"Toss you for it," said Captain Maisel. "Let's go down to the gym."

Picard gave her a very dry look. "I think I would

have to win that toss, regardless of other considerations. We can just handle your crew complement aboard *Enterprise* as well; you wouldn't have the room."

"Captain," said Dr. Crusher from down the table, "before you go too far into this aspect of the planning, it's possible I have some new information that may be of use to you."

Everyone looked at her. Picard nodded. "Doctor?"

"Well, as you say, we've been in the process of moving *Oraidhe*'s crew and caring for them. We've been moving, among other things, some pets. There were some dogs and cats, and a couple of Trill feather-apes, and various livestock—all of it unfortunately in the same condition as their owners. Obviously, the ship's vet has put them down. But there was one exception. One of the command crew had a tank of Dyan fin-crabs, and *they* were just fine."

Picard looked at her sharply. "Define *fine*, Doctor."

"They were active—alert, as far as that goes for crabs. *Conscious*, I guess, is the word I would choose, again, as far as that goes for crabs. Are crabs conscious?"

"I take it the question is rhetorical."

"Not entirely, Captain. I mean, think about it. Is a dog conscious of itself—self-aware? Seems likely enough. A cat? Almost certainly. Mr. Data?"

"If Spot is not self-aware," Data said mildly, "he provides an excellent imitation of the state."

"But go a little further down the scale," said Dr. Crusher, "and you get less certain. Are birds self-aware? Depends on the bird, I suppose. Insects? Probably not. They come very close to exhibiting nothing but instinctive behavior. A crab is barely more than an insect. These crabs were alive, and still going about their business, eating, sleeping, making more little crabs . . ."

"I'm not quite sure what you're getting at, Doctor," said Maisel.

"One answer fairly jumps out at me, Captain. They're not intelligent enough to be self-aware. They don't have the kind of highly developed associational networks that other biological life has. The apparent effect, if not the actual cause, of the condition of all the people the intellivore has attacked, is that their associational networks appear to have been stripped of associations, even the most basic ones—producing something like the most profound imaginable schizophrenia, coupled with complete catatonia. But crabs *have* no associations, at least not the kind that store memory or have active thought 'in' them. If the intellivore does genuinely drain or feed on those parts of the mind-body system that are strictly associational, the places where memory and experience and emotion and thought live—I say nothing of storage—then there's a good chance that if you could avoid having associational networks when the intellivore attacked, it couldn't harm you."

Picard stared at her. Dr. Crusher was actually smiling at him.

"It's a nice theory, Doctor," Picard said, "but I would hate to have to test it with my crew."

"You won't have to, Captain," Crusher said, and actually grinned from ear to ear. "It's been tested already, with someone else's."

"What?"

"When we were evacuating *Oraidhe*'s crew," Crusher said, "we found one person whose mind still works."

"Doctor," Picard said, resisting the urge to shout, "why didn't you let me know about this earlier?!"

Crusher laughed out loud, the first such happy sound that Picard had heard in some days. "Because the client didn't wake up until about three-quarters of an hour ago, Captain, while I was still getting ready for this meeting. When we brought him aboard, he was still unconscious like everyone else. He had been in *Oraidhe*'s sickbay. He suffered a concussion just before we found the pirate vessel—he actually fell off a levitator pad while he was putting up decorations for a birthday party. He was seriously concussed, and since good medical usage militates against interfering with the unconsciousness 'process' in cases where there isn't some overriding physical need, the ship's surgeon was letting him stay unconscious and heal at his own pace. He was still unconscious when *Oraidhe* was attacked. He woke up a little while ago, wondering where he was . . . and about three of my staff fainted."

"What species is he?" Riker said.

"Homo sapiens," said Beverly.

"By falling off that levitator," Riker said softly and with some admiration, "that man may have saved a couple of thousand lives."

"If one or both of our ships, Captain," said Dr. Crusher, "is going to attack the intellivore, I would think it needs to do so while everyone is unconscious. That's the only way we can be sure of surviving this encounter."

"Are you suggesting that we run this attack on automatic? I wouldn't care for that too much. Too many things that can go wrong . . ." said Maisel.

But Data was looking at Crusher, and she at him, and their expressions were those of two people in perfect sync. "No, Captain," said Data. "What the doctor is suggesting is that all the human, biological intelligences should be unconscious. And the pets as well, of course."

"Of course," Crusher said.

Troi opened her mouth and closed it again. "Data," she said then, *"you* have associational networks. Granted, they're made of metal and plastic and silicon rather than complex proteins. But their structure is similar enough. Can you be so sure that the intellivore won't sense you as clearly as it seems to be able to sense us, and control you as well—wipe you clean like the *Boreal* and *Oraidhe* crew?"

Data looked at her for a moment. "I would say the risk is acceptable," he said. "My associational networks have a very significant difference from yours: they are self-repairing, can repair themselves at considerable speed even during the process of being damaged, and have redundant backups. Material can be shifted around my mind from one area to another, even while a given area is being attacked."

"Assuming they're not being attacked all at once," said Troi.

"Assuming they can be attacked at all," said Crusher. "I think Data may have something here. If he manages the attack on the intellivore—"

"Physical logistics would be something of a challenge," said Data. "Since I cannot physically occupy all the necessary stations at once, I would have to be 'wired' into ship's computers."

He looked at Geordi. Geordi nodded. "It's a fair amount of work, but certainly it can be done; we have some of the necessary interface equipment preserved from previous missions."

"So what's being suggested here," said Picard, "is that everyone on the attacking ship would be rendered profoundly enough unconscious so that when the intellivore attempted to drain their minds, there would be nothing perceptible there to drain."

"I can do that, Captain," said Crusher. "Drugs

are the best way. I can control the length of unconsciousness, and the depth of it, with great precision."

"Nothing in medicine is ever that easy, Doctor . . . or so you keep telling me."

"Oh, there are dangers. I can *almost* flatten an EEG. It's not wise to leave it that way for long; brain tissue gets lazy. I would prefer not to leave it that way for more than an hour, several hours max. But certainly this operation wouldn't take that long."

"I would hope not!" said Picard. He looked at Data.

Data shook his head. "From beginning approach to completion, certainly no more than an hour."

Troi looked at him with concern. "There's still a danger," she said. "Speed of self-repair—well, you know your rate for that. But it's going to be difficult to quantify the amount of power with which this thing might hit you. If it hits you with too much—" She shook her head. "Your positronics might be wiped clean, no matter what you can do. And then the intellivore will just wait until everyone wakes up again, and drain them dry."

The command crews looked at one another. Picard sat quiet for a moment. He looked at Troi, glanced away, then at Crusher, who gazed at him steadily.

"Let's get ready to do this," Picard said.

"Captain," said Ileen, "now, *this* is not quite suicidal any longer. I think this is my job. My crew is smaller; we have fewer supernumeraries among us than you have. They're all people who know the dangers associated with—"

"As does the crew of the *Enterprise*," said Picard. "No, Captain." Ileen raised her hand to object, but Picard interrupted before she could begin. "First of all, we need backup. Your ship is lighter, more maneuverable, and under some circumstances faster than ours. It makes sense for you to be the backup. If we fail, another ship will be needed to keep tailing that planet, at a safe distance, while calling Starfleet for help and making sure other ships don't come near until that help arrives. The other reason, the main one, is that we're better bait." Picard's smile was grim. "There are more of us than there are of you. We're a bigger mouthful, a tastier prize."

Maisel smiled back. "Sweet reason I knew about," she said after a moment. "This must be the sour kind."

Picard nodded at her concession. "Believe me, Captain, if this fails, you'll have a chance to indulge your desire to master the moment's challenge. You're going to need all your speed and wit to save the situation. You have an enemy out there worthy of you. So do we. And—" He paused and gave her a rather dangerous grin. "I wouldn't complain too loudly, if I were you. We may be the ones to administer the coup de grace, but *you're* going to be the bait for the polar bear, the initial distraction that will give *Enterprise* a chance to get in close. *You're* going to put yourself out in the open where that planet will hope to be able to take a stab at you . . . and then you're going to run like the devil. You'll have thought screens, but they won't be turned on until about a tenth of a second after the intellivore tries to start working on you. We'll handle that: Data will have your command codes. And in the few moments that it's distracted . . . we'll come in and give it a little surprise."

Ileen smiled. "I've never played chicken with a planet before," she said. "You thought of that just now, while we were sitting here? Remind me not to play Go with you."

"I shall." Picard looked around. "Ladies and gentlemen, it appears we have a job to do. Let's go see to it."

Chapter Eight

THERE COMES THAT TIME when a captain, having
commanded, must get out of his crew's way and let
them work. Picard knew it. There were times,
though, when it was very difficult. This was one.

Nonetheless, he restrained himself valiantly
from going down to engineering, where Geordi and
Data were making antimatter and struggling with
the screens. He kept himself out of sickbay; the
single survivor of *Oraidhe* would most likely be
struggling with his own grief and confusion at the
moment, and the sight of the *Enterprise*'s captain
might not help him. He even got off the bridge,
where Riker and Ileen Maisel and Frances Pickup
and a few others were doing the detail work, the
tactical planning, on the broad strategic plan that
Picard had sketched out for them.

However, because he found that he desperately did not want to, he took himself down to the cargo bay. Or, more accurately, he now had to spend a little time judging which one to go to. There were four of them now, aboard *Enterprise* anyway, and two on *Marignano:* huge rooms full of mats, and silent people, empty eyes looking up in the light, people being turned to one side or the other, to keep the pressure of their bones from burrowing through their skin over hours and days. Intradermal feedings, quiet care . . . and the medical staff of two ships moving quietly from person to person. The staff spoke in murmurs, as if not to wake the sleepers. But there was no chance they would awaken.

Beverly found him, as it happened, long before he thought to look for her himself. For a while they just stood together, looking at the room. He said, "How are you doing . . . you and your people?"

"Better than last time," she said. "Doing something always helps."

Picard nodded, looking around. He paused, then said, "Where's Clif?"

Beverly shook her head. "He's gone," she said.

Picard looked at her in sudden shock.

"He had his release requirement on file," she said. "Everything was in order. And this is exactly the kind of condition for which it was intended. When all this is over, you'll want to schedule a ceremony for the disposition of the bodies."

Picard nodded. "When this is over."

They walked a little. "Do you think we're going to pull this one off?" he said.

She glanced at him sideways. It was almost a sly look. "I think we have a chance. If we don't . . . we'll certainly have very little time to think about it." She raised her eyebrows. "If anyone can pull this off, though, Data can. As for the rest of us, we'll be sleeping sweetly."

They walked a little farther. "I think that's the part of it I hate most," Picard said.

Another sideways look. "The loss of control . . ." Beverly said.

Picard nodded. "Not just that, though. Would it sound too childish to say that I'm really going to miss the action? The adrenaline rising, the excitement of it all happening . . . the adrenaline's going to rise, but there'll be no point. I'll either wake up to find that we've won . . . or wake up and find that we've lost. Maybe I won't even wake up at all. And the adrenaline won't help, no matter which way it goes."

Beverly chuckled softly. "Childlike, not childish," she said. "Hardly a pejorative. You're just another norepinephrine addict. At least you can admit it, though."

"The first step to recovery, eh? What's the cure?"

"Usually more adrenaline," Crusher said, with a very slight smile.

"Thank you very much, Doctor," Picard said, dry.

"Don't mention it . . . you'll get my bill in the morning."

They walked on down the rows of mats. "It has to be said," said Beverly. "I should apologize to you. I got pretty righteous with you the other day."

Now it was Picard's turn to give her the wry look. "You know something that Jack used to say to me?"

"No, what?"

"He said his father had told him that the most important thing to remember in a relationship was that if you were ever proved right about something, you had to apologize immediately."

Beverly laughed. "So he did. I always did run a little late, though."

"I wouldn't worry about it. Better to be late that way than in the more final sense of the word."

"You're probably right about that, too."

Picard glanced around them at the *Oraidhe* crew who lay about, feeling once more the heaviness that had been sitting in his chest all day, like a stone. "All this would not have happened if I had moved a little faster."

"You can't say that, Jean-Luc. There's no guarantee, no way to be sure; too many variables in the situation, as Data would say."

"The truth is," Picard said, "that not all your trying to argue me out of how I feel is going to make any difference to them."

Beverly looked at him with compassion. "No,

you're right there," she said. "It doesn't. But that doesn't make what I'm saying any less valid. You called it: you did your job the best you could. Sometimes people die." She stopped at the head of a line of mats, looked down along it. "In fact," Crusher said, rather coolly now, "to be perfectly accurate about it, *always,* people die."

"That sounds a little defeatist, Doctor."

Crusher shook her head. "No, there come times when the ability to accept what is means a lot more than striving to make it otherwise. That poor guy who fell off the levitator: if it weren't for *Oraidhe*'s surgeon leaving him alone, accepting his condition and letting it be as it was, right now we might not have a prayer."

"You would still have found the crabs."

"Yes, and would you want to have based a strategy on *them?* You should have seen your face. It looked like you were thinking, *Crabs? Crabs??*" She chuckled again.

"I suppose you were right. How *are* the crabs?"

"Pregnant," she said, "both of them. We're going to be coming down with fin-crabs momentarily. And I could use some help in finding them good homes."

Picard gave her a lofty look. "Talk to Commander Riker. He handles all my pet placements."

Crusher snorted softly. They looked over the big room together, and Beverly said, "When will we move?"

"Data says he needs another six hours to make sure all of the nonessential personnel are transported. Geordi needs about the same. A little extra time to get our resources properly divided between *Enterprise* and *Marignano* . . . and then we send the intellivore formal defiance. If it, or they, acknowledge it, fine. Otherwise, *Marignano* moves out and starts the active part of the operation. And Mr. Data will follow."

"I've got my staff and *Marignano*'s getting ready measured dosages of entaskamine-lauryl," said Crusher. "Logistically, it's going to be a little exciting on both ships, but we'll manage it. We have a lot of volunteers, and spray injectors aren't difficult to use."

"How long will you need?"

"Twenty minutes from the word *go* will be more than sufficient."

Picard nodded. "I'll give you an hour's warning so that everyone will be in position."

"That'll be fine, Captain."

He started to move away. She put a hand briefly on his arm, and he paused to look at her. "When did you eat last?" Crusher said, with considerable mock severity.

"I don't have any appetite, Beverly, really."

"I understand." Probably she did, but Picard could just imagine what else Crusher was thinking on the subject: probably something a lot less tactful, and indeed, he'd often enough given her cause.

177

He opened his mouth to agree, but never had a chance. "Your blood sugar must be down in your boots, though. *Eat!* That's an order. A sandwich, a milkshake, I don't care . . . just eat."

"I will. I have something to take care of first . . . but I will."

Picard walked away.

Down in engineering, a big, blocky pod assembly had been erected not far from the main warp emitter coils. Engineering crew were circling it in a wary way, as well they might have: inside it was nearly a cubic meter of antimatter.

There was a control panel off to one side, and Geordi La Forge was lingering over it like a mother with a sick child. Every now and then, he would look up from the panel and take his pulse to see if it had gone down any. It hadn't. He was very nervous.

It's all very well to talk about siphoning antideuterium slush around by the hektoliter, like so much beer moving from the keg to the tap. But the amounts usually used in any given day are reckoned by the microgram—amounts that could not only fit on the head of a pin, but could hold square dances on it. People tend to become blasé about the kind of energy produced by the total annihilation of matter and antimatter. Geordi was not blasé about it. He knew.

So it was with trepidation, but also a certain amount of excitement, that Geordi had gone down to the pod access area on Deck 42 and run about a cubic meter of the antideuterium slush into a magnetic bottle. He had taken his time about it; the failure of the magnetic field around the bottle, even just enough failure to let a single atom or particle of conventional matter into the antimatter while it was being transferred, would have given a new and less strictly astronomical meaning to the term *big bang*.

It had to be walked back to engineering, since it wasn't really practical to put antimatter through the transporter. Slowly and with care, Geordi and one of his staff had taken the big bottle back up to engineering on a levitator pad, and people had looked out their doors at it, as it passed, with very dubious expressions indeed. Apparently, word got around this ship even faster than he had thought.

The engineering staffer helping him was Lieutenant Farrell. She was a young, cool-looking blonde, with a wicked theoretical sense; subatomic physics was her preferred field. She glanced back at some of the people who were watching them, and said under her breath, "You'd think they thought we were going to drop it."

"Please . . . don't even *think* about it."

They got down to engineering without incident, and now stood at the control panel together, looking at the tank by the warp coils, set up where they could watch it and work on it in comfort . . . if *comfort* was the word.

"You and I," Geordi said, "are going to be mad bombers."

"I think we've got the mad part right," she said, when he explained to her what they were going to be doing. "Isn't it bad enough having this much antimatter out of the containment tanks in one lump—"

"Lump?" Geordi looked rather scornfully at the tank they were working on. "That's slush. That's not a lump . . . yet. But it will be."

"So will we, pretty soon," said Farrell, shivering. The tank's refrigeration, needed for the supercooling required for the magnetic fields, chilled the air for a yard or two around.

"See," Geordi said, "the problem is that if you're going to stick an antimatter bomb into a large body and then expect it to blow up, you can't use it in slush form. Slush sloshes. It's unstable in its own matter configuration, and it'll produce unpredictable annihilation results if it's not stabilized. You'll get an uneven energy output curve when it blows: one side of the explosion might be stronger than the other, the planet won't crack evenly . . . and then where would we be?"

Farrell shook her head in a resigned way as Geordi peered through the viewport. "You make it sound like you're baking a cake."

"Yeah, well," Geordi said, still peering, "I've been in a few cooking classes now, and I did a pretty good angel food last week. When all this is over, I'll give you the recipe . . . or I might even make you one."

"I like the way you say *when* all this is over," Farrell said, coming around the panel to look in through the port herself.

Inside, she could see the slush becoming much less slushy. The antimatter was floating in the middle of the pod, squeezed into a spherical shape by the magnetic fields there; and the squeezing was getting harder—there was an antitractor field working in there as well. "See," Geordi said, "it's all just a question of balance. This is going to be completely spherical when it's done; there won't be as much as a millionth of a degree of eccentricity. And that's just the way you want it. You keep an eye on that eccentricity; that's your job while I watch the pressure. That's going to get pretty cranky in a little while."

"Right," Farrell said, and came around to sit at the panel and watch the shape of the forming, contracting sphere. "It's actually developing some color, isn't it?" she said as Geordi took another look through the port. "There's a little blue in the silver."

"Yeah," Geordi said. "I've seen that before, but never as intensely as we're going to see it now."

"How dense are you planning to make this sphere?"

"As dense as it can be," Geordi said.

Farrell began to get twitchy. "You mean you're

going to strip the atoms down to the component particles?!"

"Oh, no, why bother? That wouldn't make any significant difference. But we *are* going to pack it right down to metal."

"Metallic antideuterium!"

It was certainly doable. Any of the gases, if exposed to enough heat and pressure, can be made liquid. Tougher are the solid states: no gas really wants to become a metal, at heart. But that was what this was going to be.

"It's going to make it a lot easier to handle," Geordi said.

"It's going to make it a lot easier to *drop,*" said Farrell.

"And a lot less bulky."

"Mr. La Forge," said another of his staff, a tall dark man with a pronounced Scots burr who put his head around the corner from one of the nearby side bays, "Mr. Data says he'd like a word."

"Right. Keep an eye on this, Farrell. Remember, zero eccentricity—"

"Yes, sir," Farrell said. She looked at the tank and shivered, for reasons having nothing to do with the refrigeration.

From around the corner came La Forge's voice, sounding surprised. "What," he said, *"again? . . .* Well, all right, Data. Farrell? Get someone to relieve you. You're wanted . . ."

She waved over a passing lieutenant, told him what was needed, and went off after Geordi.

On *Oraidhe,* a single form walked the corridors, not quickly—silent in the silence, head bowed a little, alone.

She was in energy-conservation mode, as might have been expected: lights dimmed, the usual sounds of an active starship muted almost to nothing . . . but that was to be expected, for the thing that made a starship most valuable, its living population, was missing. All the doors were closed; the silence in the halls was one that Picard had heard on his own ship, very occasionally. Even at the most benign of such times, when it was in orbit around Earth or linked to some starbase for a refit, and almost all the crew were missing except for the skeleton crew working on her, he disliked the sound of the vessel in such circumstances. She was like a body with no mind.

Which struck rather painfully to the heart of the problem.

It took him a little while to find the holodeck; *Oraidhe*'s design was rather different from *Enterprise*'s. Outside the door he stood for a moment, then touched the programming controls. The computer queeped softly and then said, "Ship's systems are in conservation mode. Operation of this facility is restricted."

"Override," Picard said. "Check voiceprint."

"Overridden," the computer said after a moment. "State desired function."

"List available programs linked to Captain Clif," Picard said.

He waited a moment. The computer showed him a listing, and he saw a name Clif had mentioned. "Run Arken One."

"Program is running. You may enter when ready."

Picard stepped forward; the doors opened, closed again behind him.

The ridge was scattered with boulders of a bluish stone. *Basalt?* Picard thought. *Or just a high cobalt content, maybe?* The ridge trended upward against a sky that was blue-green, not as a freakish meteorological phenomenon, like a prestorm mountain sky on Earth, but blue-green naturally. All around, high mountains hemmed in the outer view.

There was no growth here, whether because of climatic conditions or simple lack of life-forms to fill the specific ecological niche, Picard couldn't tell. At least the pathway up the ridge was clearly marked: someone had come along and put startlingly white rocks among the slate-blue ones to mark the route. Picard went on up, getting into the rhythm of the climbing and the breathing, breathing deeply enough to make sure he got the air he needed.

The trail was one of those that seems simply to vanish at the top. Around him, the mountains screening the exterior view began to fall away very quickly, as Picard slogged on up the trail, his breath coming harder now. *Still out of shape, a little,* he thought. *Or maybe just recent stress. Dr. Crusher is probably going to have words with me about needing more exercise—*

He came up to the top of the path. It did indeed simply stop, abruptly falling away on the far side of a little patch of bare stone with some flat rocks placed on it here and there.

And beyond it . . .

Mountains. Nothing but mountains. They flashed with snow, the nearest ones; glaciers draped themselves over their shoulders, some demure as white veils under their snow cover, some glittering with sunfire off blue-white ice and polished stone. Some were sullen and gray, deeply wrinkled with crevasses, dangerous-looking. Here and there, between one of the mountains and another, you might catch the slightest hint of blue-green, the idiosyncratic cyanophyll of the Trill homeworld, laid in a thin layer over the unforgiving stone.

Picard turned slowly in a circle, looking in astonishment for anything that was *not* a mountain, a glacier, or a cliff. Finally, behind him, looking down the ridge by which he had come, he looked away over the near-endless mountain crests and saw something else: the sea. A deep rich color, almost royal blue, it lay there under the brilliant sun, but too far away to see the glitter of the light on its surface. Just a bloom or glow of pale bright light was sheened across it, half faded away in the mist hanging over the mountains that lay between.

"Quite something, isn't it?" said Clif.

Picard turned. Clif was coming up over the far side of the trail, from where it dropped off on the opposite side of the mountain's "tabletop."

Picard took a couple of long breaths, as much from the climb as anything else. "I would have thought you might be up here to meet me . . ."

"No," Clif said. "The first time anyone climbs Arken, he should do it alone. It saves the need to think you have to say something to the other person while you're trying to take it all in."

Picard nodded.

"I thought you might be along when I wasn't available," Clif said, sitting down on one of the flat stones, "so I left this for you. How do you like it?"

Picard shook his head. "It's an extraordinary vista," he said. "Hundreds of valleys . . ."

"Thousands," Clif said. *"Ayai'leh-hirh,* the Five Thousand Valleys. This is one of the largest mountain ranges on any inhabited planet."

"Not the kind of place that would ever be heavily settled," Picard said, looking away across it: mountain after mountain, like the sea, seemingly endless.

For a while they sat in companionable silence. "I'm sorry for giving you the preprogrammed version of the two-credit tour," Clif said, "but you know how the schedule's been. We'll do this properly when there's more time."

Picard's heart seized. He had to be quiet for some moments. Finally, he managed to say, "You know, I just remembered. I keep meaning to ask you what *'Oraidhe'* means, and then things keep knocking it out of my head."

Clif laughed, a little ruefully. "It's one of these mountains," he said. "Look south a bit. See that pointy one there? No, not the one that leans left, the one just past it. That's the one." He stretched, then leaned back in the sun, his legs stretched out in front of him. "There was a battle there once, in the valley under the mountain," Clif said. "One of the city-states in the nearby lowlands was trying to dominate the mountain people; the mountain folk had fortified the valley, intending to defend it or die. So they defended it. The battle was one of the epic kind—huge imperial power meets and breaks on smaller independent band of free people."

"An old story," Picard said softly. "Is there a motif for that one?"

"Yes," Clif said. " 'Live free, or die.' "

Picard nodded. "Ileen made me laugh," Clif said. "She told me that *Marignano* was something similar. An interesting coincidence." He sighed, looked southward. "But sitting up here," he said, "it's hard to believe it all ever happened. The sun shines, the wind sings its usual note, or goes quiet. You can't imagine the noise of a battle, people hitting each other with twirl spears, hacking each other into pieces. Only the beasts of prey remind you, when you see them occasionally, the big prowling carnivores that work these mountains. They're as happy to take advantage of a free feed as they are to catch something themselves. Happier, in fact. The local people know the tendency. Those mountains over there"—he pointed off a little to their left—"are all named after predators. Ilrienh, Noraikghe, Sethe. 'Bear Mountain,' your people might say, 'Lion Mountain'." He shook his head. "My people gave them enough feeds, up in these parts, in the ancient days. But at least now we've stopped doing it, and the mountain can just be the name of a mountain. In fact, probably most Trill alive don't even know the name *Oraidhe* now as anything *but* the name of a mountain. Possibly a sign of some success on our part. Thank the Powers, we've been spared as a species to see what lies farther along, on the other side of the mountain, in the next valley over . . ."

"Clif."

The Trill looked at him.

It was almost impossible to say it. "I'm so sorry I killed you."

Clif looked at him from above, a slightly quizzical expression. "But, Jean-Luc, if something happened to deprive me of capacity, you know I have a release on file; I wouldn't have left you much choice. And if it's by action or inaction you felt you've killed me, then I'm sure you had a good reason. You did it defending your people, or *Marignano,* or both; or all those other lives off behind us, back in the warmth, nearer the heart of things."

Picard looked at him through eyes that smarted. "I'm not sure how we're having this conversation."

"You started it," Clif said. "But one of the captains I studied under at Academy always used to say, 'Preparation is everything. Whatever else you do, anticipate.'" He looked out over the mountains. "If you've come to this particular piece of dialogue, you may have come to it for comfort. I don't know that I have any to give you . . . except to say that I would probably have done the same for you." He laughed softly, then. "Except that maybe that's *not* much of a comfort."

"I only wish that this were real."

"Reality . . ." Clif gave him a dry look. "Shall I ask 'What is truth?' and wash my hands? See," he said, "I'm well read in your culture."

"You know what I mean."

"I suspect I know what you *think* you mean. It's not happening in the real world, so the understanding doesn't count. Is that the line of reasoning? If you're hearing this, if you're giving me answers that are evoking these responses, then believe me, the understanding *was* real." He turned a slightly annoyed expression on Picard. "You might give me credit for that much, at least."

Picard was quiet for a few moments.

"I know," Clif said. "It's the holodeck edition of the Pathetic Fallacy. The loaded question: should you be polite to what isn't human, or doesn't exist, just on general principles? Your choice. It won't matter, finally. You have work to do, probably more work than ever, if I'm dead. You'll probably have to go do it, shortly. All I can do is wish you luck . . . and know that I 'really' did, before . . . as well as now."

He held out his hand to Picard. "How real does reality have to be, Jean-Luc?"

Picard looked at the hand for a long moment, then took it and shook it.

"Gods' speed, Jean-Luc."

Slowly, he got up from the stone and, without looking back, walked on down the ridge and out of the holodeck.

On the bridge, from the center seat, "Report," Picard said.

"Mr. La Forge has completed his work on the device," said Data. "It is loaded into one of the photon torpedo tubes and is ready to be launched."

"Very good. I see that your own equipment appears to be ready."

This was a fact nearly impossible to miss, since Data's station was now a nest of additional optic cable and various black boxes; a framework to support more cable had been attached to the back of his chair. "Yes, Captain. Mr. La Forge is on his way up to assist with linking me to the ship's systems."

"All right. I take it you've had unnecessary systems taken out of the control loop."

"No, Captain. We are still uncertain about the intellivore's ability to read our own interior activities. I have decided it is safer to make no changes for the moment."

Picard nodded. "Very well. Status of the intellivore?"

"Same course, Captain," Riker said, "same speed. It seems quite content to let us run after it, for the moment."

"That's excellent," Picard said. "And possibly that's evidence that it has not yet been able to tell what we're up to." He looked over his shoulder as La Forge came in. "Mr. Worf, you have the necessary linguacode message ready?"

"Yes, Captain. It requires the intellivore to cease the attacks on any ships or planets in this area, and to leave at best speed." The look on his face suggested that Worf very much hoped that it would not. "I will regret, however, missing the battle that will follow."

Picard let out a breath. "That goes double for me, Mr. Worf, but it would seem, for a change, that the best and only way for us to achieve victory in this particular fight is to go to sleep, a requirement that most fighters of the past would probably envy us. Picard to Crusher—"

"Here, Captain. Are we ready?"

Picard looked around at Riker and the rest of the

bridge crew for any dissenting opinions. "I would say so. One thing first. *Marignano*—"

"Here, Captain," said Ileen Maisel's voice.

"Are you ready, Captain?"

The laugh that followed was just a touch nervous. "To have my brains drained? I'm not too sure about that."

"I pity the poor creature that tries to drain your brain, Ileen. Operationally, are you ready?"

"Yes, sir. We've got the thought-screen generators linked into the shields, though since we're not going to be testing them, we have no idea whether they'll work."

"If Mr. La Forge installed them," Picard said, "they'll work."

"I should make you put money on it. Meanwhile, all nonessential crew are now aboard *Enterprise.*"

"Then we'll proceed. Everyone aboard will be unconscious within an hour from my mark. Doctor Crusher—"

"Ready."

"Mark. Action will begin at an hour and five minutes."

La Forge came down to stand beside Data, and peeled away the "hair" from the back of his head, revealing the small, glittering, telltale lights that acted as diagnostics for the positronic interfaces. "I've done three sets of checks on the hardware," he said to Data, "and everything seems to be in order. Let's get you hooked up and see how it feels."

Geordi lifted one of the more delicate cable connections and plugged it into the back of Data's head. Data blinked. "That connection is patent."

"Good. Now the weapons system interface—"

Geordi clicked it in place. Data's face worked oddly for a moment.

"Don't sneeze," Riker said.

"There is no reason for me to do so," Data said. "The weapons interface is functional."

Data froze where he sat.

Geordi looked at him with some concern. "You all right, Data?"

"I am functioning," Data's voice said, but it came from the annunciator system, not from his throat. "I judge that it would confuse matters if I try to operate my body and the ship at the same time: it seems wiser to run one or the other."

"All right," Picard said. "Data, you, too, should probably try to behave as much like the ship itself as possible, for the time being."

"I have been doing so, Captain. In any case, external effects such as speed and course are not being altered."

"Good."

And that said, there was nothing much more to do but wait.

After about half an hour, Crusher came up to the bridge with her medical bag. "All right," she said. "Who wants to go first?"

No one moved. Everyone looked at everyone else.

"I," Picard said, "will be *last.*"

"Before *me,*" Crusher said, "yes."

It remained very quiet. "All right," Crusher said. "Everyone sit down and get as comfortable as you can. Mr. Worf—"

"I will remain at my post," said Worf.

"Mr. Worf," Dr. Crusher said as kindly as possible, "not even Klingons can remain standing while unconscious for prolonged periods. Sit down before you fall down. On the floor, if you want to, or over here by the captain, I don't care."

"Doctor," said Troi suddenly, "I'll go first, if you don't mind."

Crusher stepped down by Troi, looking at her sympathetically, and picked the correct dose vial out of her bag. She leaned over Troi and said, very softly, "Getting noisy, are they?"

Troi gave her a small, unnerved smile. "You don't know the half of it. But it's not just that. It's becoming . . ." She looked around and down toward the rest of the ship. "So *quiet* down there . . ."

The spray injector hissed against Deanna's arm. She blinked for a moment, then leaned back against her seat, her eyes closed.

Crusher watched her carefully. "Good induction," she said. "Next?"

"Captain," Data said suddenly—or rather, it seemed as if the ship said it, in his voice. Everyone looked up in alarm. "Sir, the intellivore is beginning to decelerate."

"The balloon's going up!" said Captain Maisel's voice from *Marignano*.

"Mr. Worf," said Picard, "send that message. Then take your shot."

"Aye, sir," Worf said. He worked at his panel for a moment.

Picard sat rigid. *Your last chance,* he thought. *Don't make us do this—*

"No response," Worf said softly.

"Give it a moment, Mr. Worf."

The moment went by, and another one, and another.

"It's decelerating *hard,*" Maisel's voice said. "Starting to alter course. Toward us."

"Don't let it preempt you, Captain!" Picard said. "Carry out your orders! Doctor—"

"Right. Medical teams!" Crusher said. "Finish up, stat. Company's coming!"

"On my way. Good luck, *Enterprise!*"

Worf sat down hurriedly beside Picard, across from Riker. Beverly was with him in a second; the spray injector hissed, and he slumped. Then she moved to Riker, then La Forge, and then out of Picard's sight.

"Mr. Data," Picard said.

"Captain, the intellivore is turning toward us at warp six."

His heart was racing. *It should not end like this. Oh, don't let it end like this.*

"Carry out your orders, Mr. Data. And take good care of my ship," Picard said.

From behind, Crusher hit him with the spray injector.

Against the sound of *Enterprise*'s engine note changing, scaling upward for the first time in many hours, the world went hazy around Jean-Luc Picard. Life went dark . . . and then stopped being life altogether.

Chapter Nine

ILEEN MAISEL WATCHED with mingled excitement and horror as the planet grew and grew in her viewscreen. *Then felt I like some watcher of the skies/when some new planet swims into my ken,* the back of her brain misquoted. And *this* one was swimming a lot too fast for her tastes. *Chapman, honey,* she thought, *if you'd have seen this coming toward you, you would have left town in a hurry.*

"Coming in fast, Captain," McGrady said. "Accelerating, but not too much. It's going to try to take us into its warpfield."

"Then start playing around with ours," she said. Maisel turned to Pickup. "Frances?"

"Right, Captain."

"Make enough ripples in the field so we'll be a tough catch."

"No problem, ma'am. Executing now—"

The ride immediately got a lot bumpier. "Oh, great," Ileen said. "We're all going to need to have our teeth worked on after this one . . . assuming we're lucky enough to get away at all. How's your luck running?"

"One of my ancestors won big at something called a casino," said Pickup. "Three hundred years ago . . ."

"Oh, *good,*" Ileen said. "Thanks so much."

She watched the planet creep closer, and wondered what had triggered the sudden move. *It must have picked up something from comms,* she thought. *Or maybe even from the computers. We still don't understand how it manipulates signal the way it does.* But it was moving fast now; the intellivore plainly had decided that the passive mode was no good. It would attack, eat them all if it could—

"Closing, Captain. It's going to be in range very soon. Thirty seconds—"

Something was tickling at the back of Ileen's mind, and inside the back of her head, it seemed, a feeling like she had to sneeze with her brain. Part of her wanted to scream, for the feeling was wildly abnormal—her brain did not normally sneeze—and she thought she knew what it heralded. "Mr. Data," she said, "here it comes! Frances, Paul, fight it the best you can."

And she began thinking, as hard as she could, of the most aggressive, destructive, nasty thing she could think of right away. It wasn't hard; her mother had always told her she was a violent little monster. "Straight at it, Paul," she said, thinking the thoughts with force, as if they were bullets or beams. "Get that deep scan going for Data!"

"Scanning, Captain—"

"And then we're going to eject the warp core."

"What??"

"You bet," Ileen said. *Believe it, you bastards. You want to play chicken with starships? Fine. You're going to blink first.* "And we're going to dump all the antimatter at the same time." She started making frantic "I'm only kidding" gestures at McGrady. "That scan, never mind that it's not complete, feed it to *Enterprise, now!"*

McGrady obeyed her, but while he did so he stared at her as if she was out of her mind.

And then she *was* out of it.

Everything froze. That planet kept swelling, swelling in the viewscreen. She could not move a muscle. And there was something in her head . . .

The presence grew. When she was young and had first started studying space travel and the history of it on Earth, she had laughed at the stories of alien abductions, of people claiming things had been done to their bodies and minds.

This, though . . . *this* was the real thing. It was as if something looked at her out of the darkness, as if something stood behind her. And it gloated. It was amused. She knew, she could feel, that it had watched and seen, if vaguely and through a curtain of somewhat warped context, that she and the others traveling with her had set themselves against it, that she would try to stop it from doing what it wanted.

It did not deal in words, or at least none that she could translate. There was an effect in the back of her mind, not like a sneeze but like a great bell, tolling, clanging deep and out of tune. But the feeling that went with the tolling, the knell, was amusement, laughter; it thought she was *funny*. And outrage, too—that she should dare to try to stand in its way.

Something was happening to her mind. It was changing . . .

Slowly, Ileen came to understand that she was food . . . and someone was hungry. Someone wanted her more than anything. There was something old, wise, sad out there, asking for help. She was the difference between sorrowful extinction (and the bell tolled) and blessed survival. Her sacrifice would be remembered. Centuries, millennia from now, when other species were dying out, *she* would be remembered as one who had made a difference, who had preserved life, who had kept her oath. All she had to do now was give herself up. It was better, it was easier. Soon the world would chill down again, would go cold and ordinary. Soon she would be free to move. And when that happened, all she had to do was activate these controls, in this order, to bring that other ship under her control, do to it what was needed—and she could be back in this sanctified state again, give herself up to what would remember her forever. It would happen very soon. She must wait, be careful. Otherwise, she would do great harm to the old, wise life that was beseeching her for help. *Wait, be true, be faithful.*

And the world flickered—

On the *Enterprise,* Data heard the tolling.

The earlier parts of the experience, leaving aside the basic danger of the situation, had been pleasant. It was a little unusual to *be* the ship, to feel power and signal flowing through him, inputs and outputs chasing around after one another. He had wondered briefly if having a nervous system felt like this.

Data could sense the slight creak in the hull and the support structures as velocity changed, as skin fields and stress fields remolded themselves, changing their geometry to better suit the new speed. The sensation of this huge, powerful body, taking care of itself, was quite intriguing.

The only thing to mar it was what he must use that "body" to pursue. The sense of that huge, deep voice, slurred, untranslatable as yet, was far back in his mind at the moment. It was a good question whether he was hearing it through his own positronic networks or through the ship; for there was a kind of resonance between the electronics of the ship and of the planet which was growing bigger and bigger in the viewscreens.

He watched it come. At one level, with a great clinical detachment, he was impressed by the technology that could produce so steady and well behaved a warpfield; the planet's oceans, what was left of them, were staying mostly in their beds, though there was some understandable turbulence which even gravitic dampers would not be able to handle. But it was surprising.

Then, though— "Here it comes, Mr. Data!" said Captain Maisel, seemingly inside him. The two ships were still data-streamed together. Hearing the warning, on which he and Maisel had earlier agreed, he cut the link between the two ships. He would not need it for what he was about to do.

The milliseconds ticked away; in the ship's bones, they did the same. Data plunged forward, feeling space bending around him, atoms shattering into their component particles against the forward-curving skin of his warpfield, sleeted around him, trailed away behind. There was a burning in his chest: the matter-antimatter reaction pumping the warp flux through into the engines like blood on fire. Ahead of him, *Marignano* trailed what became, in sensor view, a luminous track of particulate and plasma vent as she dove toward the planet.

Data watched. For him and for the ship, at the experience speed they shared, it was less a dive than a slow snowflake fall. Behind *Marignano,* starlit, the boss of its north polar cap now swinging around into line, came the planet, the intellivore.

Data and the *Enterprise* were no more than two hundred thousand miles away at the moment. The intellivore planet had dropped out of warp now and was decelerating. He could see the gossamer shimmer of space bending around the planet, striving to cope with the suddenly present mass: local gravitic influences being warped all awry, the delicate lines of force burst through as carelessly as cobwebs, stinging against *Enterprise*'s shields like hair-fine wires as they broke and lashed their way down into lower energy states. In his mind, as if in his hand, Data held the control codes for *Marignano:* a key, ready to be used. He reached out, fitted the key into the matrix lock that was waiting for it, and turned it.

The code flashed from *Enterprise* to *Marignano* on the covert channels—

—and the key stuck, and would not turn.

He re-sent the code, turned the key again. But the door did not open; there was no response. There should have been a flood of information for him, released scan from *Marignano.* Nothing came. Something was blocking it at its source.

Marignano and the planet were very close, no more than thirty thousand kilometers now. Twenty—

"Captain Maisel," Data said down the comm link. "Captain Maisel, please respond."

No response. *I left them unprotected too long,* Data thought. *It has drained them . . .*

He had a plan ready for such an eventuality, as

much at Maisel's insistence as at Captain Picard's; they had known that the intellivore might be too powerful for even their best plan to deal with, and that there might therefore be no scan result. He would have to pick a likely spot on the planet, use phasers and photon torpedoes to dig a hole in it, then plant the bomb and run. And it might not be effective. If it failed—

He shifted course, plunging not directly toward the planet now but in a wide arc around it: an orbit at two hundred thousand miles. His own scan would not be terribly effective at this distance, but it would have to do. He began calculating the trajectory at which he would emerge from his scan pattern, and reached inside himself for the codes that would arm the device.

—and, as promised, the world went gray and chill. That kindly presence faded away, and Ileen Maisel found herself staring at the glowing, growing presence of the planet in her front viewscreen. *There,* whispered the voice in her mind. *Remember what you must do. Help us, save us . . .*

She reached out to the console to help the sad voice. It would never be sad again.

And in the back of her brain, like a tickle, something said, *Chicken . . .* Only a whisper, weak—

As if it were the last thing she would ever have a chance to do, she threw herself at the conn, hammered in a new course setting, implemented it. The ship wrenched violently off to one side, and shook and rattled and shrieked as she flung it back into warp, out into the dark again.

Pickup and McGrady were slumped by their posts. "Oh, dammit, dammit," Ileen muttered, but there was no time for them right this second. She staggered back to the comm console, hammered on it. "Mr. Data!"

"Captain Maisel!" he said.

Maisel had never heard emotion in his voice; what she heard now was at least considerable urgency. She pounded in new settings on the comm board, implemented them. "Here's that scan. Good old stubborn software, it got it all even when that bloody cue ball was trying to interfere with it!"

"I thought we had lost you, Captain."

"I thought you did, too."

"Are the thought screens holding?"

"Just. We had a field flicker—it had us for a moment, knew it was going to lose us . . . but it was sure it would get us again. That arrogant— Never mind." The feeling of the sneeze was still tickling at the back of her mind. "I don't have time for analysis, you're going to have to do it."

"Analyzing data now, Captain. Originally a very standard planetary structure, except that there have been extensive and unusual modifications to the planet over—"

He stopped.

"Mr. Data? Mr. Data!"

* * *

He saw what the ship saw, what *Marignano*'s sensors had seen. Strange to be reading his own sensors at the moment, and also reading *Marignano*'s, two sets of eyes looking through two different sets of vision at the same object—

The upper crust of the planet was riddled with tunnels—mighty diggings, very old to judge by the sensor readings, caverns artificially extended, galleries, halls and passageways a mile wide, through which huge conduits passed.

Some of them were carrying antimatter.

There were engines. They were made of no substance that Data recognized. *Where did this planet come from?* he found himself wondering.

Old did not begin to describe it. The planet was ancient, even as the most ancient species of this galaxy would reckon such things. And built into it was a warp engine, or rather a system of warp engines, of a size and structure that Data had never seen or even imagined. He could detect little in the way of detail—there had been no time—but the gross detail, warp coils, the shape of the warpfield, the way it was generated—of all those things he took note. He noted the gigantic pools of antimatter trapped inside the body of the planet/vessel, storage pods like the *Enterprise*'s but far more massive. They were scattered under the crust in what were probably the most stable configurations that could be found, reinforced with more of the alien metal that was everywhere. The planet still had a molten core, but it was still very small, and sealed inside a spherical shell of that metal, the refractory qualities of which were staggering.

Some eight hundred pools of antimatter, scattered here and there. Some of them were from five to ten cubic *miles* in volume; and a massive system of conduits that serviced all those pods led to the huge main engines buried in the mantle of the planet.

It had been a cold planet once, Data thought. Someone had found it, come to it, worked it over—"chopped and channeled," he could just hear Geordi saying. The captain had been right. In this regard at least, in terms of the intellivore's venue, there had been choice. Someone had built this planet to wander, equipped it with so much antimatter that it would be tens of thousands of years, possibly hundreds of thousands, before it needed to refuel.

Idly, part of his mind that was not busy being the ship now turned its attention to the calculation. *Eleven-hundred-forty-point-three cubic miles of antimatter,* he thought. *Antiwater, rather than slush deuteriun—interesting, that. Annihilating with equal amounts of matter—*

—at which point something began to happen.

His mind began to change . . .

Data could actually watch it start to happen. Other parts of his mind, as yet unaffected, stood aside and observed the mechanics of it, the way a bystander at a stage magician's performance will stand in the wings of the theater, and at that angle see what the people out in the orchestra cannot: the card vanishing up the sleeve, the scarf with the bird in it tucked up behind the jacket . . .

To the affected part of his mind, the image of the planet swelling in the viewscreen was now beginning to fill with a terrible pathos. There was trouble there, danger. Life was dying. Help was needed. But there was also danger in remaining in orbit. He must break away the part of the ship that could land, and bring it down to the planet's surface, where it would be safe, it and its many people who slept. There the old intelligence, the endless knowledge that was stored on this planet, could be saved, preserved, put aboard *Enterprise* and taken away for the good of billions of people alive now, and billions more yet unborn. He must hurry. There was danger; that was why the planet had fled out of the dark. There was something coming, meaning it harm—and these other ships, too, they would all be destroyed. He must be swift, land quickly, help it save the knowledge, the old wisdom . . .

Data watched the "confidence trick" spreading through his mind, or trying to. For this eventuality he had been somewhat prepared. *You have associational networks,* Troi had said to him. But at the moment, he was running several "sets" of his mind in parallel. The effect was odd: he heard echoes every time he thought. He was surprised, though, when he sensed something like a sudden surge of power from outside himself, and another of the redundant minds fell to the influence that was working on the first.

Data tried—subtly, he hoped—to dislodge the influence that was acting on his "outer" mind. It would not be dislodged.

So he did something inelegant, and perhaps catastrophic, but (he thought) necessary. He shut that mind down.

The influence on the other part of his mind—the part still occupied—increased. He let it do so, watching it, again as if slightly from the side.

And then, quite suddenly, the influence was gone. To that part of his mind, the planet was simply the intellivore's again, and the wisdom of the ages nothing but an illusion.

And then the pain came crashing down.

He would have thought this experience was impossible for him. "Like describing color to a blind man"—he had heard the saying often enough. Often enough, he had tried to get people to describe what pain was; and their descriptions, though obviously profoundly meaningful to those doing the describing, to Data only sounded like some terrible kind of fiction—stories of a body turned against its owner, out of control.

Now, though, the intellivore explained pain to him . . . and it used others' pain to do it.

How many lives had it taken, over all the long tale of years? *It* knew; that was the horrible thing. It could number every one. It *kept* them. Maybe not the energy itself; that was long consumed—that undetectable effluvium from which it derived, not energy, but pleasure. And their memories, their pain, it ate that, too. And it kept the memory of that pain, as a gourmet will keep labels from wine bottles in a book, and take the book out every now and then to look at the labels and say, *"That* was a nice one."

For if there was one thing the intellivore had not been in a long time, that was alive. Once, he suddenly knew, it had been many—telepathically connected, a long time ago. Not exactly a hive mind, not exactly a clone group, but an old species of many millions, their minds partly joined, partly independent.

They had begun to die as a species, becoming unable to reproduce. Some of them did not want the species to die, at any price; that was how their new turn of life had started, in the earliest times . . . the fear and rage of some of them infecting the whole species slowly, over time.

They had an extraordinary technology, it was true. While wandering down the byroads of that technology, one of them least pleased with the option of seeing both himself and then his species pass away discovered something—a slightly new version of a legend occurring on many planets: that by devouring the energy of others' minds, one could trick one's own mind out of the knowledge of its own mortality. The mind forgets; only the body needs to be convinced, then, that life will go on forever.

The members of that old species who first used this technique found out what to do. But first, while the new science was still being developed, they preyed on one another; and when that became a danger, they preyed on other species. They went out in ships for the hunt. That was a mistake, for other species followed them home, and wrought such revenge on their world that it was considered unwise to try that again for a while. They kept quiet, and preyed on one another as they had been doing—such behavior had settled itself into their culture as permissible now, even respectable. Then someone found the next step in their evolution.

They would build a world. They would live on it, and move it as their whim pleased them. They would go where they liked, and take what they liked. And if anyone became difficult, tried to fight them, then they would simply withdraw for a little while, taking themselves away off into the darkness. Then as now, in space, distance was the best defense.

They built the planet. It was the work of a thousand years. They built matrices that would hold their disembodied intelligences safe and immortal. As long as there was power at the heart of their world, they would continue . . . and they made sure that they had a power source that would never fail them. Finally, they poured themselves into the matrices they had prepared, took up residence, and went forward into the night, seeking whom they might devour.

211

There were already many fewer of the intellivores than there had been a thousand years previously. All the weak of the species had been devoured. The minds left swimming in the formlessness of the matrix inside their world were the hungriest, the cleverest, the ones most in love with their own lives and the taste of others' minds and thoughts—not merely to experience but to consume. They did not stop improving their world, once they were out among the stars; they devised the field that automated and powered the business of the devouring.

From world to world they went, in that other galaxy from which they originated. They gourmandized there for millennia. And when there was no life left there, they set out into the darkness. They had the power they needed to survive, and the memory of many minds that they had stripped. But new thought, fresh life, was sweeter, and they looked forward patiently to the patch of light before them. They watched it develop into a spiral as they approached, and the spiral into a great cloud burning with stars; and they knew that here was a bigger galaxy than theirs, younger, burning hotter. There would be life here in abundance. They would devour and devour, and it would be long ages of pleasure yet before they devoured it all. It was laid out before them, theirs for the taking.

The sensation of pain grew worse as it came closer to Data, seized on part after part of his mind, the influence spreading again, pain growing more terrible and unavoidable. He had no defense against it, no previous experience of pain to help him know how to cope, and now his reaction was like that of a human child who feels the cut finger or the scraped knee for the first time, and can feel nothing but horror and betrayal at the cruel universe that allows such pain to occur. He floundered in it, not knowing how to fight, and the pity and anguish for the billion victims twined together in him—

Data felt himself drowning under the weight of it. Soon there would be no him anymore, only it/them, and it would have its way with everything. For *this* possibility, too, Data had made a plan. There was no telling what would happen to the *Enterprise. But I have no choice—*

Before the intellivore could tell what he was doing and react, Data programmed himself for a tenth-of-a-second shutdown . . . and implemented.

Everything went black—

—and then *white.*

He blinked and found himself staring at the screen, which had whited out. "Mr. Data!" yelled Captain Maisel. "Are you there?"

"Where else would I be, Captain?"

"Oh, Lord, you're infuriating sometimes. *Are you all right?*"

"The hold the intellivore had on me is broken. I

have your scan, Captain." And then he added, *"You* are responsible for my recovery."

"You did something first."

"I shut down."

"I hoped you might, even though it was a risk. I've been sending *Enterprise*'s command codes at you for the past couple of minutes."

"Is that all it has been?" Data said softly.

"That's all. But I got your screens up, just the visual-light function. The thing doesn't like it; it backed off a little. Don't just sit there, Data, *go* for it, before that thing pulls another trick out of the bag!"

Data reached back down inside himself to his connection to the heart of the ship, and made a shift, a change—

On *Marignano,* Ileen was still standing, hanging on to conn, staring at the screen—and the little sphere of light in front of them suddenly went so blindingly bright that the violence of it actually made her stagger where she stood.

"He's back in the saddle," she muttered. "I'm getting out of range. Paul? Get up, Paul!"

Her exec was staggering to his feet. "You all right?" Maisel said.

He looked at her, his face haggard. "I'm never drinking out of *that* bottle again."

"You and me both. I need you working, now. Frances, get up!"

Pickup reached up to a nearby chair and pulled herself upright. "Captain, what—"

"We had a little run-in with our nasty friend there, but it didn't finish the job. Don't tell me," Maisel said, hurriedly holding a hand up. "I won't tell you mine if you won't tell me yours. Take the conn. Get us out of range, and bring us around in a big circle. Mr. Data's about to start digging, and I want to be in a position to help him if he needs it."

"Look at that," said McGrady. The screen had backed way down in intensity, as a matter of self-defense. *Enterprise* was pumping something like eighty percent of her warp engines' output through the screens, with the instruction that they radiate in the visual spectrum.

"If that's not what a nova looks like," said Ileen, "it's a real good imitation."

"Kepler's Star all over again."

"I hope not. Come on, power those weapons up. Frances, get me a reading. What's the planet's sensor web doing?"

Pickup scanned briefly and said, "Getting flickers, Captain. Uneven spots in the planet's sensor power curve. Overloads—"

"Good," Ileen muttered. "I hope it likes it. Let's see if the things of darkness really don't like the light."

Enterprise was swinging close by the planet on impulse. The light harrowed every bit of the planet. It had been a ghost until now, silvery, misted with distant starlight, indefinite. Now it stood out sharp, became hard and real. The shallow seas glittered and bloomed as the eye-searing point of light swung around, dipped in under the ten-thousand-kilometer level; polar caps glanced the light back as *Enterprise* dived gracefully into a ball-of-wool orbit that would give it complete scan coverage, and (they hoped) blind every sensor.

A line of light shot up, just missing her.

"There we go," said Ileen. "Jean-Luc was right: it wouldn't bother shooting until its brain tricks weren't effective. Target that source. They're shooting wide—they don't see *Enterprise!* I don't know how long this is going to last; let's take advantage. Photon torpedoes and all phasers, at your discretion. Fire!"

Marignano dived in behind *Enterprise,* targeting the big phaser emplacements as they revealed themselves. Picard had been right—they were awesomely powerful. However, they were missing. And when they fired, you could see where they were . . . with enjoyable results. *Let's just hope Data doesn't blunder into one of them. And that they don't anticipate where he's going to be,* Maisel thought.

Pickup took careful aim, fired three photon torpedoes at once, and took one emplaced laser out. She targeted another emplacement, used two torpedoes. The emplacement stopped working. She kept firing, peppering any emplacement that showed any action.

—And suddenly, under them, the planet started to move again.

"Uh-oh," said Ileen. "Mr. Data! It's accelerating!"

"Noted, Captain—"

Aboard *Enterprise,* Data could feel the itching, the tearing at the back of his mind again. Still blind, the planet was trying what had worked on him once before, and trying it with increased force, and it was actually having some effect again because the *Enterprise* was so close.

Tractors, he thought, and the ship obeyed him, flinging out the most powerful tractor beam it could manage at the planet. At one spot, where the photon torpedoes from *Marignano* had blown through to substructure, the tractors found purchase and hung on.

Marignano came up fast behind, matching speed. "Point-five-six," said Pickup down the comm link. "Five-eight. Six—"

"Don't lose it!" Data heard Ileen say. "Paul?"

"I'm on gunnery, Captain. Targeting live emplacements—"

Data saw one of the emplacements blown right out of the planet's surface, then another, and another. "Point-six-four," Pickup was saying. "Point-six-five."

"Mr. Data," said Maisel, "what are you going to do?"

"If the planet goes to warp, I shall go with it."

"Not if he keeps up like that, you won't."

And it was true enough. Looking through the

scanners' "eyes," Data could see that the planet was altering the shape of its prewarp field.

"I hope I didn't give it that idea," Captain Maisel said somewhat ruefully. "If you're going to stay in warp with someone you've got a tractor on, you're going to have to conjoin warpfields. If you can't—"

"When the planet goes into warp," said Data, "the *Enterprise* would certainly be blown loose, possibly destroyed by the warp conflict resonances."

Not that the *Enterprise* cared for this treatment in the slightest. Where her prewarp field and the intellivore planet's intersected and were trying to match phase, ripples of resonance conflict were already propagating out into the adjacent screens and fields. The ride got rough. "Captain," Data said, "this is going to require all my attention for the moment."

"Okay," Maisel said. "You take care of him, and I'll dig you a nice hole. Any preferred spot?"

"Your scan shows virtual longitude eighteen east, virtual latitude forty-four—that spot is equidistant between four separate antimatter 'pod' locations. Here is a diagram of the conduit structure—" He data-streamed it over to one of Maisel's screens. "I urge you, Captain, not to breach any of those structures when you dig."

"Mr. Data," said Maisel, "I'd sooner put a thumbtack on the seat of God's easy chair."

"Point-six-five," said Pickup, "point-six-seven, six-eight—"

"Perhaps you might start digging, Captain," Data said, as gently as possible, turning his attention back to the prewarp field.

"I think I'm going to do this one myself," said Ileen, and she headed for the weapons control console. "Frances, take the conn. Keep us oriented, keep us still relative to them."

It was not as easy as it sounded. The planet began to rotate, yaw, and roll as it went, trying to add as many new sets of variables to the problem Data was solving, and Maisel could feel that maddening itch at the back of her mind, threatening to get stronger again.

"I don't like this, Captain," McGrady said. "Even with the thought screen, that thing's trying to dig through."

"Yeah, well, I plan to do a little spadework myself," Ileen muttered, programming Data's coordinates into the weapons console. "Just keep us in sync, and if that thing goes into warp, make damn sure you know which way it went." She locked a phaser collimated down to practically a yard wide onto the spot Data had indicated. *Please, whoever's listening,* she thought, *please don't let there be any antimatter conduits down there that aren't marked on the diagram. Otherwise . . .*

Otherwise, it *would* be Kepler's Star all over again. She didn't want to think about it. "You match that spin now, Frances," Maisel said, getting her phaser ready. "Keep me steady over that spot."

"Acknowledged, Captain."

Ileen fired.

There was an initial explosion from the planet's surface that made her flinch for fear of what she was certain would follow. It didn't follow. A hole began to appear, and deepen. "How far down do you want this, Mr. Data?"

On *Enterprise,* Data had his hands full—not that he had hands at the moment. The intellivore was getting scared, and its fear was making the fluctuations in the prewarp field more random. This was making his job harder. *Point-seven-six cee. Point-seven-eight—*

I am fortunate, Data thought, *that the planet is so slow on impulse. But it has never had to be fast, until now, and its difficulties with its beam weapons suggest that it has not had much need for them, either. It has become rusty.* "Ten kilometers will do, Captain," he said. "Once the bomb is emplaced in the upper part of the mantle, the explosive and shock effects will propagate right through it, whether the antimatter pods are breached or not."

"But they *will* be breached, Mr. Data. Won't they?"

"Almost certainly. Captain," Data said, "I must emplace the bomb before the intellivore goes into warp—otherwise, it and the *Enterprise* will be trapped together, and attempting to break out of the conjoint warpfield will destroy us, though possibly not them. That would be an undesirable outcome. Once you have finished digging your hole, I encourage you to be elsewhere, at great speed. The explosion should be . . . memorable."

"Mr. Data," said Maisel, "you and I are entirely of one mind in this matter, with one proviso: *you* have to do the same, and in one piece."

Data could feel, with the ship's sensors, the bodies that lay quietly sleeping around him on the bridge, and the many others all through *Enterprise*. "That is a foregone conclusion, Captain," Data said.

"Point-eight," said Pickup's voice. "Point-eight-one. Eight-two—"

"I'm digging, I'm digging!" Ileen said. The phasers had run into a whole level of that refractory material, and it was giving them trouble. "They've got goddamn reinforcement here at crust level—"

"Don't worry about the collimation, Captain," said McGrady. "Give it multiple banks."

"I said I wasn't suicidal. I refuse to start contradicting myself at this late date." Nonetheless, Ileen fastened another phaser onto the spot. It, too, collimated down as tightly as it would manage, and the two of them went to work. She started to see a red glow from the refractory material. "Getting some results," she said, and added another.

The prewarp field of the planet flickered and jumped, dimpled and smooth and dimpled again all over, like a golf ball. It began to develop that long, whiplike tail that Maisel had noticed earlier. Data, hanging on via the tractor beam as if by his fingernails, flickered and wrinkled his own prewarp field to match. It was not going to work. He was going to have to let go before he went into warp.

Hurriedly, he launched the torpedo that carried Geordi's device, snagged it with another tractor beam, and held it ready to emplace. "Captain—" he said.

"You just hang on," said Maisel, sounding harried.

"That is precisely what I will not be able to do much longer, Captain, if—"

"There we go!"

There was a sudden spit of red light from the planet below—not phaser fire, but magma leaping up. "Right there, Mr. Data," said Maisel.

"Point-eight-seven," said Pickup's voice. And then, sounding more alarmed, "Eight-nine, nine, nine-one—"

"Mr. Data, get out of there!"

He killed the tractor.

He was not expecting, however, the one that lanced up from the planet and caught *him.*

And then, almost immediately, the tractor let him go.

"Get out, Captain!" he said.

And silently, to the place at the back of his mind that burned with growing pain, and someone else's astonishment and rage—the intellivore's—he said, *This is theirs. And now it comes back to you. But then . . . space is curved.*

Marignano had spun on her vertical axis and was fleeing. Warp six—eight—nine— He saw the rainbows trail away behind her as he arced away himself in the opposite direction, pushing all the consciousness he could spare into the warp engines as if he were physically running a race. Warp five. Six. Eight. Eight-point-nine—

He heard the scream. If a sound could be said to be blinding, this one was—the scream of pain, and rage, and disbelief. It had tried so hard not to die, for so long. It thought it had succeeded. And to fail now—even now, it didn't quite believe it. Even now, it—

Terror.
White.

Everything went white. The light alone could not have physically pierced the hull, but with his eyes and his skin all sensors at the moment, it seemed as if it did. Then came the shock wave. He experienced the pain of it in his body, all along his chest and stomach and some along his back—ripping, melting pain. He fled. He fled blind. He did not know where he was going; it was good there were no stars or planets anywhere nearby.

The world remained white for a very, very long time. *Is this a sensor malfunction,* Data wondered, *or have I burned out some part of my own posi-*

tronics? At least it was not shutdown, the closest thing to death. Shutdown was dark, or rather, had no color. *But perhaps I am now sense-blind. I wonder if the condition is reparable.*

There was nothing to do but run, and keep running, and wait.

After a long time, Data thought he saw the faintest darkening of the white, and he could hear a faint hissing sound. "Mr. Data—"

The voice was very faint and far away, staticky, thin.

"Mr. Data—"

"Captain Maisel. You have survived."

"So have you. Will you for pity's sake slow down?"

"I have been unable to tell whether it is safe to slow down."

"Well, it's safe. I wouldn't slow down *much,* though. There's a big cloud of plasma behind us, and it's not finished annihilating itself, not by a long shot."

"I am in sensor whiteout, Captain. I cannot tell where I am going."

"Your present heading is three-thirty-eight-mark-four, plus two. You just keep heading that way . . . decelerate gently. I'll come up behind you. Our sensors overloaded, too, but you should get yours back in a while."

"I do not know, Captain. My situation was not like yours."

All the same, the world was graying down, getting darker. He hoped that was a good sign. He waited quietly for some while.

And then, from behind him, came something that so shocked and startled him that he nearly cried out. "Mr. Data," Picard's voice said, a little slurred, a little blurred. "I see we're still here."

"Yes, Captain," said Data. "I briefly had some uncertainty regarding the issue ... but we are here."

"And the intellivore—"

Data was silent.

"Are you all right, Mr. Data?" said the captain.

Data kept silent for a moment more, then said, "I know now what pain is, sir."

Now it was Picard's turn to be still. Data could not see his face yet, or anything else, even though the world kept graying down. Red alert sirens were whooping in the background; it surprised Data that he had not heard them until now.

"Ohhhrgh," said Riker's voice, "the noise. We can't be dead; heaven is quieter than this."

"On your feet, Number One," Picard said. "Mr. Data. Damage?"

"Damage to decks forty-two through thirty-eight—fortunately, our own antimatter pods were spared. But we have serious hull ruptures in the lower and upper decks of the secondary hull. I fear we have many casualties, Captain."

"I would say," said Picard, "so has someone else."

"I would say so, Captain," Data said.

Chapter Ten

"ONE HUNDRED FORTY-SEVEN, dead, Captain," said Riker, very wearily. "Thirty-two on *Enterprise*, all the rest on *Marignano*."

The conference room was very quiet. It was a quiet caused not so much by shock as by weariness. The two days between the present moment and the intellivore's attack had been extremely busy.

Around the table were seated *Enterprise*'s command crew, along with Dr. Crusher, and *Marignano*'s bridge crew, minus the senior conn officer, who had been killed in the aftermath of the explosion.

"We'll be ready for the ceremony later this evening, Captain," said Riker, glancing down at the padd in front of him. "Twenty hundred."

"Very well." Picard looked down toward the

other end of the table, where Captain Maisel sat, looking as subdued as Picard could ever remember seeing her. "Captain?"

"We'll be holding ours at twenty-two hundred."

"Very good. I'll be there."

Silence fell for a moment or two. Then Picard said, "Status of the repairs?"

"All the hull breaches have been mended," Riker said. "We have, though, sustained some major structural damage. When the intellivore blew, it gave us a kick in the pants of a kind that starships don't usually survive."

Mr. La Forge nodded. "Fortunately, because of Data's good offices, the ship was on a very specific heading at the time, rather than tumbling; otherwise, the shock wave probably would have shredded us."

"All right." Picard turned to Crusher. "Doctor?"

"Besides the death due to trauma secondary to the explosions," Crusher said, "we had two fatalities due to the drugs used to induce unconsciousness during the attack. One of them appears to have been an atypical allergic reaction. In the other case, the EEG never recovered after having been flattened. The cause is indeterminate."

Picard nodded.

"Something else, though," Beverly said, "has been producing some concern. A lot of people have been reporting nightmares—painful, frightening ones. Many people have trouble remembering these when they wake up, which may be a good thing. There have been so many of these reports that I find it difficult to attribute them to posttraumatic stress syndrome as such. I would suspect that in some cases, these people's unconsciousness may not have been as completely profound as I would have liked, with the result that they experienced some of the kind of thing Data went through. Other beings' memories . . . other creatures' suffering."

"Will the effects fade, do you think?" Captain Maisel said.

"I'd like to say I thought so," said Crusher, "but I just don't know yet. I've been prescribing mild sedatives or alpha, or both, for those continuing to complain of problems. So far, these treatments seem to be effective. We'll just have to keep an eye on everybody."

"We will."

"Meanwhile," the doctor said, "our other patients remain unchanged. There were some of my staff who were half hoping that once we found and killed what had sucked these people dry, they might all wake up, but I'm afraid that particular fairy tale just isn't going to come true." She smiled, just a small smile, and very sad. "Starfleet has been alerted. We'll be spreading these people among a great number of different facilities specializing in human neural and neurophysiological problems. We'll discharge our patients to the emergency medical facility on Starbase Four-forty. It's on our way."

"Yes," Picard said. "Those orders have come

in—we'll be there in about two weeks, and we'll be dropping off *Oraidhe* with them as well, for recommissioning as a new vessel. I think that name is probably going to be retired. Meanwhile, Mr. Data, how is your report coming along?"

"I will be finished with the initial report in two more days, Captain," Data said. "I received so very much sensory and other information from the intellivore that a complete record will take rather longer. And it is very fortunate that I was directly linked to the ship's computer and memory facilities at the time, for much information had to be stored there as overflow."

He was quiet for a moment, as if organizing his thoughts. "What is certain, though," Data said, "is that the intellivore was directly responsible for very many more attacks than we had suspected. For a very long time it preyed on planets in this area as well—moving in close to them without any particular concern about tidal effects—and in many cases, it slowly destroyed entire species over the course of months or years, either as a result of natural disasters secondary to the tidal effects, or by its own predation. The decline of a number of the older alien races in this part of the galaxy, which we could not understand, was directly attributable to the actions of the intellivore. So Captain Maisel's present mission, at least, is now complete: the source of many disappearances is solved."

"I wouldn't know about *complete*, Mr. Data," Ileen said, giving him a slightly covert look. "There are still some old planets around here that could use mapping."

"You mean," Picard said, with a slight smile, "that you would appreciate some peace and quiet."

"Well," said Captain Maisel, "yes. We didn't suffer the same kind of structural damage that you did—the head start Data gave us saw to that. So there's no particular reason for us to go running back to the center of things. And I would like to do some more looking around up this way to check for other signs of the intellivore's involvement. There are quite a few empty planets up this way that have shown evidence on mapping of odd tidal effects, as if a 'grazer' or planet trying to be captured had had a close encounter with them." Her expression turned slightly grim. "Under the circumstances, I would start suspecting such planets of having had intelligent life, and I'd want to examine them a lot more closely. That will be the rationale I give to Starfleet to avoid being recalled . . . and I think they'll probably respect it."

"I suspect they will," Picard said.

"There is this to consider as well," Data said, "when Starfleet debriefs us. The intellivore was indeed getting ready to change hunting grounds. Two forces existed balanced in it: a desire to remain secret and the desire for more food. For a long time the first had remained paramount, and this behavior had caused it to downscale its predations a great deal; colony ships and wandering spacecraft would, in its earlier days, have been considered very poor fare, hardly more than scraps and crumbs. The peculiar multiplex personality existing inside the planet's memory matrices was beginning to shift emphasis, however. The parts of its 'mind' intent on remaining undiscovered were beginning to lose their arguments with those parts that felt it was time to rove more widely and 'eat' better. Sooner or later—within the decade, if I am any judge—the intellivore would have actively turned inward and begun attacking the most heavily populated planets it could find. The result would have been chaos, especially since the creature was very clever indeed about working out how to exploit technologies new to it. I am certain that it would have most thoroughly 'researched' Federation science until it found ways to defend itself against nearly anything we could throw at it . . . and then the wolf would have gone out into the fold, as it were, and might have remained unimpeded—and very destructive—for a very long time. At the end, it might have taken the same kind of concentration of forces that were required at Wolf Three Fifty-nine to stop it."

Everyone sat quiet and thought about that one. "Well," Picard said, with a sigh, "it won't happen. We do know that much."

"So will a lot of other people in this part of space," said Ileen, "in a couple of hundred years."

Picard nodded. "I take it that the explosion remnant is still active . . ."

"Captain, it'll be active for *years,*" Geordi said.

"The total amount of energy released in an annihilation like that is nearly quasarlike." The engineer sighed. "At any rate, we'll let Starfleet know that this object is something that ships coming out this way should not approach closely. There's a lot of very hard radiation streaming out of that thing. If you popped out of warp too near it, you could not only burn your sensors out, but your own warp engines might react badly—energy output of that kind can adversely affect subspace structure. Also, this area is going to be a subspace radio 'blind spot' for a good while—some years, I would imagine."

"Very well . . . we'll so inform them." Picard looked at his own padd. "Is there anything else that needs our attention at the moment?"

People looked at one another. Heads were shaken. "Captain," Data said, "only this: I want to make sure that all the information I garnered from the intellivore is twinned over to *Marignano,* for eventual archival at Starfleet and distribution among the Federation's science resources. Some of it was very subjective and obscure—'memories' of planets it attacked or, in some cases, merely passed by; scraps of data about its technology . . . other such material. With extended analysis, of the kind for which I will not have that much time, the information it inflicted on me may yet do as much good as the intellivore itself did harm. It was a tremendous repository of knowledge, though it scorned the knowledge itself."

"All right," said Picard. "See to it, and use

whatever resources and assistance you need. But, Mr. Data, just one more question about the intellivore."

"Yes, Captain?"

"Are there any more?"

Data looked at him for a long moment, then shook his head. "If there were, Captain," he said, "the intellivore itself did not know about them. And I would suspect that its first intention, should it discover another like itself, would be to try to devour it as well. The life-form that the intellivore had become was most profoundly inimical to life, even its own kind—evidence of which lies in its own earlier history. When its individual parts could not find others to prey on, they would gladly devour one another. And if they had ever reached a point where there remained no intelligent life for them to devour—a point they did indeed reach in at least one other galaxy—and could neither find more nor move in pursuit of it, it is my judgment that the life-form would then have attempted to devour its own components."

"There was an old story in which someone did that," Ileen said, musing. "Some angry god punished him with hunger so terrible that he ate all the food there was, and then started devouring himself."

"B-four-one-two-four-point-six," Data said.

There were slight, sad smiles around the table.

"Yes," said Picard softly. "Well. Is that all? . . . Then, dismissed."

The bridge crews went out, but Maisel lingered a little, looking out the windows at the stars, until the doors shut.

"Something?" Picard said, rising to go and join her.

"We must be pointing the wrong way," Ileen said. "I can't see it."

Picard briefly did a course assessment in his head. "It would be almost directly behind us," he said, "if I'm any judge of these things."

Captain Maisel nodded. "Somewhere," she said, "in a few hundred years, someone will look out the window and see that, and run off to write someone else a letter. And astronomy on that planet will never be the same."

She turned away from the window. "How are *you* holding up?" she said.

Picard stood looking out that window as well. "I would be lying to you," he said, "if I said 'all right.' It has been, well, a rather energetic week. And one of our good ones has been lost . . ."

"Yes," Ileen said.

She let out a long breath then and looked toward the window again. "I can't get it out of my head," Ileen said, "that I was responsible for that, that I should have anticipated what was going to happen. Clif would laugh at me, of course, and tell me I was being juvenile and self-aggrandizing, and about fifty other things. But sometimes I wonder if this is the kind of thing that prevents them from sending starships on very many task-force missions. In situations where there's so much danger, it's too easy to look at yourself as the youngest one, or the oldest one, or the smartest one, in a given group, and to start saying, 'I should have seen that coming,' or 'I moved too fast, I should have taken more time to think,' or whatever."

Picard looked at her with considerable surprise, but he did his best to keep his face fairly still. "Ileen," he said after a while, "you can't believe that. Not really." *Because it was my fault . . .*

"Bets?" Ileen said.

Picard looked at her. "Captain," he said, "listen to me. You, better than most of us, know the dangers of operating way out here on the fringes. Without fail, sooner or later something comes along that's completely alien to human experience, and that you're not able to handle, for lack of resources, or luck, or even just anticipation. When it happens, all you can do is keep going, keep yourself and your people breathing, and get on with the parts of your work you *can* do. You did that. I did that." He swallowed. "As far as he was able, *Clif* did that. He fell, doing it, but the circumstances in which he fell will not happen to anyone else, because of what *we* did, after. That particular menace, which hadn't even been identified as such earlier, is now done forever. You know, I think, that Clif would have found the price acceptable. Well, it's harder for us: we have to pay it over and over again, in our memories. But the best way we can honor *his* memory is by continuing to do our work with a good will, because he would be unhappy with the knowledge that things were going any other way on his account."

Ileen had been looking out the window again. Now she looked at Picard, dry-eyed and frowning. "I hate it when you're older-and-wiser," she said. "I always did."

"And *I* hate it when you don't *listen* to me being older-and-wiser, you insolent pup," Picard said. "You never did."

For a moment, they just looked at each other. Then Ileen laughed, very softly, and so did Picard.

"All right," she said. "All right. I'll probably feel awful again tomorrow, but that doesn't change the fact that you're right. Dammit."

"Insubordinate," Picard said. "I think he would also have said 'insubordinate.'"

Captain Maisel smiled a crooked smile. "Yes," she said. "Well, come on. We both have memorial services to run, good cry afterwards optional. Then, later . . ."

"We'll be running together for a day or so more," said Picard. "Let's make it tomorrow."

Captain Maisel nodded; they went out.

The sky was just lightening at the fringes when, much later, he stepped on deck. There was a light breeze blowing; it sang softly in the rigging, and the morning was so quiet that the sound of the same wind stroking through the trees of the island a mile away could clearly be heard, a whisper with words in it, but no telling which words. Above the western horizon, the moon hung fat and golden, ready to slide under.

The deck rocked a little in the slight swell. Picard, in Starfleet uniform, stood there and looked down the length of the deck. The gun crews stood ready. Mr. Moore, also in Starfleet uniform, stepped up to Picard and said, "At your pleasure, sir."

"Strike the colors," Picard said.

Other crewmen, not assigned to the guns, stepped up to haul down the signals: a man's name—two beings' names, actually—and the two-flag sequence for "death aboard."

"Make honors," said Picard softly to Moore.

Moore turned, signaled at his crew. There were no shouts; no word was spoken. Of all gun drills, this one was silent. The first gun fired at the moon, in a cloud of smoke and a great spurting of sparks from the black powder, nearly as much from the touch hole as from the muzzles. The air whistled as the cannonball whipped through it.

A pause, and the second gun fired, landward; a pause, and the third fired, toward the sea. Smoke drifted slow across the deck, stinging the eyes. A pause, and then the second group of three, slow-spaced, each waiting until the whistle and splash of the ball was gone. Picard looked through the drifting smoke, over toward where the rum bottle stood on the empty steersman's bench. A pause, and then the third group of three, slow and measured.

Picard swallowed. Then the fourth group, for it was a captain who was gone, after all. The smoke drifted by.

A longer pause, and the optional fifth group of shot, for protection, for such times as this were times when the doors of men's hearts stood open; and at such times of pain, and remembrance, there were things that waited out in the dark, to creep in and make the innocent their own.

Not this time, Picard thought. *Because of him . . . not this time.*

Silence. In it, the echoes died. The offshore breeze began to freshen, and the ship rocked as the smoke blew away.

We won, Picard said softly. *At what a price . . . but we won. Your victory, Captain . . . and a glorious one.*

Rest well.

Moore came back to him, saluted. "Sir," he said, "honors are made."

"Very well, Mr. Moore. Stand down."

The crews ran the guns back in. Picard walked down to the steersman's bench, picked up the rum flask, and turned eastward.

Blinding, a splinter of sun came up over the edge of the world. The sky began to flush rose with the swift Caribbean sunrise; and high up, singular and undaunted, the morning star burned white.

Picard tossed the rum back, flung the flask out into the waves, and, very slightly, smiled . . . before starting, uncontrollably, to cough.

From across the water, faint and suddenly uproarious, came the sound of laughter.

STAR TREK®

Klingon™

A

Warrior's

Guide

In both
English and
Klingon!

MARC OKRAND

POCKET
BOOKS

Available from
Pocket Books Trade Paperback

1192-01

Look for STAR TREK Fiction from Pocket Books

Star Trek: The Next Generation®

Star Trek: Deep Space Nine®

Star Trek: Voyager®

Flashback • Diane Carey

POCKET BOOKS
PROUDLY PRESENTS

STAR TREK
DEEP SPACE NINE ®

WRATH OF THE PROPHETS

Peter David, Michael Jan Friedman,
and Robert Greenberger

Coming Soon
from Pocket Books

The following is a preview of
***Wrath of the Prophets*. . . .**

Captain Benjamin Sisko sat back in his chair, considered the blank monitor screen on his desk, and sighed.

He liked a great many things about his position as commanding officer of *Deep Space Nine*. But there was one thing, above all, that he did not like—and that was the paperwork.

The very term suggested arcane and antiquated practices, designed to blunt the mind and deaden the soul. Of course, paperwork no longer involved the use of paper, per se. That had gone out with the invention of the computer, some four hundred years earlier.

However, the concept of the bureaucracy had managed to survive, and Starfleet was as good an example of it as any. And there wasn't anything more bureaucratic in nature than the monthly report.

Of course, that was precisely the thing demanded of Sisko at this moment. If he waited much longer, he would receive a subspace scolding from Starfleet Command.

Sisko sighed again. He would much rather be hitting baseballs in the holodeck, squaring off against some of the greatest pitchers who ever lived.

Unfortunately, the report wasn't going to go away. And he could hardly fault his son Jake for not doing his homework when the captain himself was given to procrastination. So, leaning forward again, he reached for his computer padd—

And heard a familiar feminine voice flood his office.

"Sorry to interrupt, Benjamin," said Jadzia Dax over the station's intercom system, "but we've received a vessel from Bajor. I thought you'd want to know, considering it's got one of your favorite people aboard."

Judging from the sarcasm in his friend's voice, Sisko figured it wasn't one of his favorite people at all. And among the Bajorans, there were few people he had an active dislike for.

In fact, there was really only one. He grimaced at the thought.

"Kai Winn," he remarked. It wasn't a question.

"None other," replied Dax, confirming it anyway.

"Did she give any indication as to why she's here?" asked the captain.

"I'm afraid not," the lieutenant told him. "But as always, there's a good chance she's come to see you." There was a pause. "I can stall her if you like. You know, give you time to busy yourself in some obscure part of the station. Maybe take a runabout to the Gamma Quadrant."

Sisko chuckled. "That won't be necessary, Old Man."

It still felt funny to call her that, but she *was* a Trill—a combination of a humanoid host and a vermiform symbiont. It was the symbiont who carried the memories of his friend, Curzon Dax, the "old man" who'd served as its previous host.

"Part of my job," he went on, "is dealing with the Bajoran authorities. And like it or not, Kai Winn is one of those authorities."

"Have it your way," the lieutenant declared. "But if you change your mind, I could arrange an emergency in one of the cargo bays."

The captain smiled to himself. "Thanks, Old Man. I'll keep that in mind."

Leaning back in his chair, Sisko frowned. He'd forgotten how cloyingly sweet the Kai could be when she wanted someone's help. Biting his lip, he considered all she'd told him.

"So this plague," he said out loud, filling his office with his voice, "began with a bunch of replicators?"

"That's the information I've just received," Winn replied calmly. "Mind you, these replicators were not distributed by the government. They were obtained through the most illegal of channels."

"In any case, you're saying that the disease has spread," the captain continued. "Apparently through the water supply, when some of the dying animals polluted it."

She nodded. "Apparently, yes."

"And the whole population is threatened," he concluded.

"That's correct," the Kai replied. "Our immunologists tell us we could face annihilation in a matter of weeks."

She might as well have been talking about the weather in the capital the day before. However, Sisko sensed an urgency in her that she didn't normally display. The average Bajoran might not have noticed it, but *he* did.

The captain stroked his goatee. "I'm sorry, of course, that this has happened. We'll help in any way we can."

Winn smiled politely. "Good. I knew the Emissary would come to our aid. Otherwise, why would the Prophets have singled you out?"

Sisko shifted in his chair. He'd never been comfortable with the religious identity bestowed on him by the Bajorans.

By all accounts, he'd been the first to communicate with the beings they called the Prophets—the creators of the sector's first stable wormhole—and certainly he'd made an interesting first contact. But by his reckoning, he was still just a man.

"Exactly what would you like us to do?" he asked.

The Kai heaved a sigh. "There is so much that needs to be done, I hardly know where to start. Of course, our main goal is to identify the virus and devise a cure. No doubt, your Dr. Bashir has more expertise in such matters than our simple Bajoran scientists."

"Dr. Bashir is a brilliant man," the captain agreed. "Nonetheless, what you're asking for is a tall order, Kai Winn—especially within the time frame you've described."

Winn shrugged. "If it was easy, Emissary, we would have accomplished it ourselves."

Sisko grunted. "Yes, I suppose you would have. Very well, I'll get Bashir working on it. And Dax as well."

"I am grateful," the Kai remarked. "And I am also relieved, because I know you will not fail me."

He looked at her. "The Prophets told you this?"

She returned the look. "Do you have any doubt of it?"

The captain didn't answer her question. He simply said: "We'll do our best. Can I escort you back to your vessel?"

"That won't be necessary," Winn told him. "I know the way." And with that, she got up from her chair and exited his office.

As he watched her go, he felt himself shiver. It was the way he always reacted when he brushed up against something slimy.

Sisko tapped his communications badge, establishing a link with all the other badges on the station. "Major Kira, I need to see you. And bring Odo with you."

"Is there a problem?" asked his first officer.

The captain bit his lip. "I'm afraid there is," he told her. "I'll fill you in when I see you."

A pause. "We'll be right there," Kira replied.

Sisko shook his head. He wasn't looking forward to telling the major that her whole race was in danger of extinction.

The Bajorans had fought so hard—and endured so much—to throw off the yoke of Cardassian rule. It would be a terrible and ironic shame if they were to succumb to a vicious little bug.

In her office, Kira Nerys studied the pictures of the replicator that Kai Winn had provided. She sifted through them, shaking her head and muttering to herself.

"Something wrong, Major?" came a voice from behind. She turned to see Chief O'Brien behind her. He had a box of tools in his hand.

"Just working on a problem, Chief." Her eyebrows puckered into a question. "And you?"

"You complained your office was too cold last week, remember? I thought I'd check it out for you."

"Oh, right. Fine." She paused a moment and then extended a picture to him. "What's your opinion of this?"

He took the picture and gave it a glance. "Not particularly good composition. It's slightly out of focus, and pardon me for saying so, but it should be more centered. . . ."

"I mean of the equipment pictured there, Chief," Kira said patiently.

"Oh." He paused a moment and then shrugged. "Standard replicator model twenty-one-A. Not exactly state-of-the-art, but a real workhorse. Newer models tend to break down faster. They don't make them like this anymore."

"No one ever makes anything like they did anymore, Chief. At least, that's what I've noticed." She took the picture back and said, "Apparently, it was acquired through the black market."

O'Brien let out a whistle, but then said, "Well, I guess I shouldn't be surprised. You can get anything on the black market, it seems."

"Yes," Kira agreed, "but as near as we can tell, this caused some serious problems. It cooked up some kind of virus that's . . ."

Her voice trailed off as she saw O'Brien's look. That was when she realized and remembered. "By the Prophets— your family's down there."

O'Brien nodded speechlessly and then found his voice. "We've got to get them back up here."

"We can't," Kira told him regretfully. "There's a quarantine on Bajor. No one can come out of there." She hesitated, looking for something to say. "Chief, I wouldn't worry—"

"You wouldn't worry? With all due respect, Major, it's not your wife and daughter down there!"

"No, but it's not as if I don't have friends or family there," Kira said sharply, "and they're Bajoran. So far, it seems we're the only ones affected. To the best of our knowledge, any humans down there are perfectly safe. All right?"

She wasn't sure if he'd even heard her. "Major," he said quickly, "if it's all the same to you . . ."

Kira nodded. "You'd like to adjust my office temperature later, I know. Right now you want to get a call in to your family to make sure they're okay." She waved him off. "Go, go. It's all right. Just get back here before icicles start to form on me."

"Will do," said O'Brien, and he quickly bolted from the room.

Kira sighed. Then she scanned the images of the pictures into the computer. "Computer," she said, "study the images I've just placed into memory and search for any serial numbers or indications of previous ownership."

The computer went to work, and Kira leaned forward, waiting for the results.

* * *

Dr. Julian Bashir peered at a series of screens to the left of his research station, where additional clinical data from Bajor was displayed as it was received. He drummed his fingers nervously on the monitor's surface.

Each screen charted a different bio-sign for the population already exhibiting symptoms of the disease. One dealt with respiration, another with heart rate, a third with temperature, and so on. There were details regarding the illness's effect on musculature and nervous system.

The work was remarkably exacting, considering the panic that must be spreading all over the planet's surface. But then, he reminded himself, the Bajorans were nothing if not dedicated.

Turning to another screen, the doctor regarded the Bajoran blood sample that had been transported to the station not half an hour ago. Though the sample itself stood under strict quarantine in an electromagnetic construct in the lab next door, Bashir had the feeling it was right in front of him.

An adversary, he thought. And a horrific one at that.

The virus, like all viruses, was basically a helix of DNA. But in this case, it was dark purple and—considering it was without sentience or volition—strangely malevolent-looking, as it floated in a sea of Bajoran blood. While he watched, it invaded a stray skin cell, piercing the cell wall with ease.

The white blood cells that clustered around the entry point did so in vain. They were clearly of no use against the virus.

In a matter of just a few hours, the doctor knew, the invader would force the healthy cell to expand its energies in the creation of another helix—a twin to the first one. And as the first cell collapsed, spent, the second helix would go on to invade a second cell. The process would be repeated, then repeated again, on and on . . .

Until the host body was so ravaged it couldn't help but succumb. A grisly end, to be sure.

And there was nothing exactly like the virus in his files, which included the sum total of the Federation's medical knowledge. The thing was a stranger, an anomaly.

Bashir turned to Dax, who was sitting on the other end of the infirmary, charting the spread of the disease across the face of Bajor. Though her back was to him, he could see the results of her work.

Against the greens and browns of Bajor's topography, a number of bright orange lights dotted the map. The greatest cluster was around the Paqu village, where the first outbreak seemed to have occurred. However, as the graphic showed only too well, every continent was now infested with the telltale orange spot.

No surprise there. Bajorans preferred face-to-face contact to electronic communications, so they traveled around their globe more than people on other worlds.

"Jadzia?" he called.

Dax didn't turn around. She just sat there with her back to him.

"Jadzia?" he called again.

Still no answer.

Getting up, the doctor traversed the infirmary and took up a position by the Trill's shoulder. He leaned forward, to get a better look at her.

What he saw took him by surprise. Dax's eyes were red-rimmed, almost welling with tears. And her mouth was a thin hard line.

"Jadzia?" he repeated softly.

Finally her eyes shifted toward his. There was a faraway look to them for a moment. Then they came into focus.

"Julian?" she said. She blinked a few times. "Sorry about that. I guess I wandered off for a second there."

Eyes narrowing with concern, Bashir nodded. "Are you all right?"

The Trill managed a smile. "I'm fine. Just a little tired, maybe." She rubbed her eyes.

"You can take a break," he advised her.

Dax shook her head. "No," she said emphatically. "Now where were we?"

"I was about to ask you if you'd seen any changes in the spread of the disease. Pockets of resistance, perhaps."

Returning her attention to the map, she considered it for a moment. Then she gave her response. "No change at all— though I wish I could say otherwise."

The doctor sighed. "I know what you mean."

Dax looked up at him. "How's the culturing going?"

Bashir shrugged. "We won't know for a few hours yet."

He was in the process of producing samples of the virus for testing—a hundred samples, to be exact. Like the original sample he'd received from Bajor, they were in the lab next door.

"Still," he continued, "in a way, it's a good thing that the virus grew so quickly. If it were slower to reproduce, the creation of test samples would have taken a lot longer."

The doctor eyed his friend. "You're sure you're all right?"

Dax dismissed him with a backhanded motion. "Go," she told him. "I'm fine. Really."

He went back to his work, but he could tell there was something bothering her—distracting her. He didn't have to look far for an explanation, either.

The Trill had always been a compassionate person. And she had made a great many friends among the Bajorans since her arrival on *Deep Space Nine.*

All that misery on the planet had to be affecting her. Ravaging her emotions. Playing havoc with her concentration.

It disturbed him greatly that it should be so. If he was going to come up with a cure for the virus, he would need Dax operating at her best. Her scientific expertise would be invaluable in the hours and days to come.

Look for
Star Trek Deep Space Nine®
Wrath of the Prophets
Wherever Paperback Books are Sold